THEATRE SYMPOSIUM
A PUBLICATION OF THE SOUTHEASTERN THEATRE CONFERENCE

THE UNIVERSITY OF WINCHESTER

Published by the

Southeastern Theatre Conference and

THEATRE SYMPOSIUM is published annually by the Southeastern Theatre Conference, Inc. (SETC), and by The University of Alabama Press. SETC nonstudent members receive the journal as a part of their membership under rules determined by SETC. For information on membership write to SETC, P.O. Box 9868, Greensboro, NC 27429-0868. All other inquiries regarding subscriptions, circulation, purchase of individual copies, and requests to reprint materials should be addressed to The University of Alabama Press, Box 870380, Tuscaloosa, AL 35487-0380.

THEATRE SYMPOSIUM publishes works of scholarship resulting from a single-topic meeting held on a southeastern university campus each spring. A call for papers to be presented at that meeting is widely publicized each autumn for the following spring. Authors are therefore not encouraged to send unsolicited manuscripts directly to the editor. Information about the next symposium is available from the editor, Matthew Scott Phillips, Department of Theatre, 211 Telfair Peet Theatre, Auburn University, Auburn, Alabama 36849, (334) 844-4748, phillm2@auburn.edu.

THEATRE SYMPOSIUM
A PUBLICATION OF THE SOUTHEASTERN THEATRE CONFERENCE

Volume 13   *Contents*   **2005**

4 CONTENTS

Introduction

THIS YEAR'S SETC THEATRE SYMPOSIUM was special for me for a number of reasons. Besides being the last conference for which I served in an editorial position, I had chosen a topic that I find especially interesting, and the various approaches that the presenters took toward the topic were exciting and followed lines similar to my own historical research. In addition, the presenters at this conference were varied in discipline in a way that directly reflected one of the primary goals of *Theatre Symposium*: to examine the interstices between theatre practice and scholarly inquiry to understand how history is created by both practitioners and theorists. *Theatre Symposium* has always focused on the practice of theatre and its place in its cultural milieu rather than on critical analysis of text, and that focus has endeared the conference and the journal to me personally. I have been dramatically inspired every year by the fruitful, heated, sometimes almost frantic conversations between scholars and practitioners as they encounter new information, theoretical and practical approaches, and logistical dilemmas and inevitably emerge with renewed vigor and valuable insights to take to their own work.

This year's topic, "Theatre and Travel: Tours of the South," resulted in a wide range of subject matter, and as I organized the symposium, I worried that these authors would have little to share with one another. The topics ranged from contemporary African American theatre to nineteenth-century circus to rail travel and small-town opera houses. I wondered if there would be sufficient theoretical and historical overlap to inspire dialogue. In the end my concerns were unfounded. No matter the theatrical genre or historical period, touring performance productions and the venues in which they perform(ed) share a host of logistical and societal difficulties that made the wide gaps between such theatrical traditions as minstrelsy and Gilbert and Sullivan surprisingly traversable.

An additional, unexpected coadunation of scholarship was a historiographical one. Repeatedly, issues of the creation of theory, the difficulties of archival research, particularly for genres of "popular" theatre, and the uneasy juxtaposition of theory and practice (particularly for living theatrical forms) resonated with all the presenters. We debated about how soon a contemporary form could be theorized and whether critical distance includes that of time. We lamented all the lost documents that make performance on the margins, such as tent shows and minstrelsy, so difficult to research. And we shared tricks of the historiography trade. Information about theatre can sometimes be found only by comparing such far-flung sources as railroad schedules and weather reports, minutes of town council meetings, and error-prone theatrical programs. The unexpected emergence of these discussions has influenced the organization of this volume.

The symposium, and this volume, was anchored by the work of our two keynote speakers, Sarah Blackstone and LaVahn Hoh. They each addressed the logistics and catastrophes that have beset touring performers. Blackstone concentrates on the disasters that befell tent shows and circuses—weather- and accident-oriented—and examines what those disasters can tell us about the day-to-day and business activities of theatrical forms. Hoh examines the logistics and mishaps of circus travel and connects the evolution in touring practices to changes in the demographics and desires of American audiences. The other articles selected for this volume address a distinct theatrical form or touring event and elucidate at least one of the practical and historiographical issues we discussed that weekend.

Dawn Larsen writes from the point of view of both a practitioner—she owns and operates a Toby tent show—and a scholar facing the difficulties of researching an underarchived theatrical form. Besides detailing the critical reading necessary to evaluate often contradictory ephemera, Larsen relates her own touring experiences, echoing some of Blackstone's attention to the physical hazards of the tent itself.

The next two articles concentrate on the conjunction between text and cultural context, one historically and one speculatively. Beth Osborne looks at the Federal Theatre Project production of *Altars of Steel* and how its visit to Atlanta reflected the inability of the FTP to relate to southern culture when it traveled there. Barbara Lewis looks at the more recent play *The Little Tommy Parker Celebrated Colored Minstrel Show* and how it dramatically illustrates the real-life dangers faced by black minstrel performers traveling by rail at the end of the nineteenth century.

The issues of rail travel and theatre—the innovations afforded to theatre by the railroad's appearance in the nineteenth century, the dangers presented, and the wide variety of theatrical genres that utilized it—are neatly rounded out by Jane Barnette's essay, "The Role of William James Davis in the Rise of Chicago Touring Theatre." Much of her account tracks the historiographical difficulties of marrying theatrical and railroad documents, and the article is a primer for the process of using the evidence of one discipline—rail travel—to illuminate another—theatre—personified in William James Davis, who left a career with the railroad to pursue one in theatre management.

The next two articles deal with two very different touring experiences by contemporary African American theatre troupes. J. K. Curry talks about the National Black Theatre Festival in Winston-Salem, North Carolina, calling it a "one-stop tour." Productions from around the country travel there to take part in the theatre festival and to get their work seen in the hopes of garnering further tours to other locations. Interestingly, the logistical issues that they encounter, and that the festival itself must deal with, are in concert with those endured by the other touring groups related in this volume. Almost as an answer to all the accounts of logistical difficulties, kb saine discusses the very successful tours of Tyler Perry and his Madea plays. Concentrating on Perry's relationship with his audience and the loyalty of a traditionally non-theatregoing population, saine illustrates with a modern example the benefits that traveling theatre has traditionally brought to distant and disparate audiences.

I asked Bruce Speas to contribute the last article because of the questions of historiography I discussed earlier in this introduction. The theorization and analysis of theatre in history begins with the painstaking task of gathering and compiling data. In many instances, particularly with popular theatre of the nineteenth century, no stable producing organization ever existed, and productions weren't considered "legitimate" enough to be covered by mainstream presses. Scholars must be creative in their search for information and cautious in speculation based on limited data. Speas agreed to document his research process into the Farmville Opera House. His account provides a peek into the unusual places scholars must go sometimes for information and a tour through the process of analysis.

The articles in this volume have a lot to offer the practitioners and scholars who strive to discover new methodologies for both theory and praxis and for melding the two. The authors' examinations of the logistics and accidents common to touring provide insight into undertheorized theatrical practices—their history, their present, their audiences, and their artists' inexhaustible desire to perform.

Susan Kattwinkel
College of Charleston

Twisters, Howlers, Conflagrations, and Cataracts

Traveling through a Hostile Landscape

Sarah J. Blackstone

O N OLD MAPS THAT SHOW the edge of the world you sometimes find the phrase "Here There Be Dragons." Such warnings are relevant to touring acting troupes throughout history and maybe particularly for troupes traveling in the American South in the nineteenth and early twentieth centuries. Touring is hard—always has been, always will be. The dragons can be logistical, moral, financial, bacterial, and/or atmospheric. What seems to be high ground can turn out to be a swamp and vice versa. Troupers never quite know what will happen on the road, what they'll find when they arrive, how they'll be received as they perform, or if they'll get out of town in one piece. Still, the lure of new climes, big bucks, and different customs continues to attract theatre people to the open road. For some, touring becomes a way of life, for others an adventure to experience once in a lifetime, for still others the end of the road.

Although a focus on disasters may seem a bit ghoulish to some, there is much to be learned from approaching the history of theatre through various lenses. Disasters bring the attention of the nation to specific events and locations, and descriptions of the events and their aftermath abound. From these accounts can be gleaned interesting information that enriches and deepens our understanding of the theatre and its place in society. By looking at disasters involving theatre troupes through the eyes of nontheatrical observers such as reporters, members of the community (and perhaps the audience), and troupers who were outsiders in hostile territory at the time of the disaster, the lines between touring troupes and communities become blurred, and new insights may emerge.

Such accounts give us the rare opportunity of hearing how "ordinary people" viewed the theatre of their time and how "ordinary theatre troupers" dealt with the difficulties of landscape (both natural and moral), as everyone reached a level of equality through shared hardship. Traveling new byways through the historic record eventually brings us to well-worn paths but perhaps after discovering new territory within the boundaries of the old map.

Odai Johnson recently published a very good article in *Theatre Survey* that expands our knowledge of early theatrical activity in the Leeward Islands. He argues convincingly that David Douglas's American Company was by no means the only English-speaking theatrical company touring the islands in the eighteenth century. How did he discover these competing companies? Through descriptions of a mighty hurricane that struck St. Croix in 1772. The hurricane destroyed not one theatre and its attendant company but three.[1] By researching the usual theatrical sources (playbills, reviews, and so forth) and combining these with descriptions of the devastation, Johnson confirmed the names of performers and companies and discovered the names of plays that were never presented and other useful information. He notes that no further theatrical activity is reported on St. Croix until 1775, and neither of the theatres standing before the hurricane was rebuilt. He also states that he finds no further mention of most of the members of the Leeward Islands Company after this disaster—anywhere in the New World. As is always the case, other leads discovered in the coverage of the hurricane will be followed to other "lost" information, and theatrical territory will continue to be remapped to reflect our new knowledge.

Disasters leave a rich residue of oral history as well. More anecdotal than strictly factual, this tapestry of information about how theatre enters, joins, and exits a community, how companies and communities respond to disasters (often finding each other great allies in the face of difficult circumstances), and the lessons learned from traveling add to our sense of what it is to be a theatre professional. Such travels increase our conviction that what we bring to communities "off the beaten track," and what we learn from those communities, is of great value—worth suffering for, so to speak.

Disasters come in many varieties. Let's begin with the weather because the weather can make or break a show regardless of any other factor. The southern United States (however that is defined) does not have a theatre-friendly climate. When it isn't too hot and humid to stand, it is blowing—either very hard straight at you (hurricane) or very hard in circles (tornadoes). Almost always when it blows, it rains, or sleets, or hails, or snows. When it rains, it floods. After it blows, rains, and floods, it is too hot and humid to clean up. In this environment touring shows have always had special problems with which to contend.

Weather is remembered and recorded by touring companies. Circuses and other traveling shows usually keep route books, journals of the day-to-day activities of the company. Good days are noted by the size of the gate, and sometimes brief descriptions of weddings, birthday parties, or the visit of some famous person. Bad days always take up more space and usually begin with a description of the horrible weather, a disgusted notation of the size of the gate, and a listing of injuries and sometimes deaths. Old troupers know good weather is everything to a traveling show. Billy Choate quotes his grandfather on the origin of tent shows:

> My boy, it really doesn't make any difference. When it is 6:00 p.m. and the lightening [*sic*] is flashing, the thunder is roaring, it is pouring down rain, and we are out grapevining the tent, I like to think Mr. Ginnivan was the start of all this. But when the sun is shining, the grass is green, the house is full and the leading man is not drunk, I like to think I am the one who started such a grand and great institution.[2]

Harry Webb, a cowboy with Buffalo Bill's Wild West, describes the effect of weather on a show that performs outside—with no cover for the performers and little for the audience:

> Now, a Wild West show in bad weather, it's hell, and when the weather is good, why it's beautiful. So we have good, bad, and indifferent. And then plain hell. Because when it's raining and snowing and the lot is all nothing but mud, and you're riding a buckin' horse there or anything, and you happen to fall in the mud and roll around, why by the time you got to the back end you wouldn't know your outfit.[3]

Again from Billy Choate, on the effect of weather on audience members:

> We had a big crowd and during the first act it started to rain, not a storm, just a hard rain and it didn't stop. It was raining so hard people couldn't hear what was being said on the stage, so the curtain was dropped and an announcement was made the show would continue as soon as it stopped raining. The only problem it kept raining and raining harder. In a few short minutes water was running through the tent a foot deep. The men took off their shoes and socks and rolled up their pant legs, and ladies took off their shoes and stockings and prepared to stay and see the show come hell or high water. It finally stopped raining. Even though they were sitting

with their feet in water and mud, we resumed the show and the audience enjoyed the rest of the evening.[4]

He goes on to say: "In all my years in the tent show business I have seen some disastrous situations but I have never seen an audience given their money back."[5]

Audience members were also much at risk from the weather. In circus jargon a "blowdown" means that a tent has collapsed because of wind or other storm-related problems. Blowdowns are greatly feared. Roustabouts and troupers alike are careful to describe the proper rigging of the tent in stormy conditions. Because of the weight of the canvas, tents are rarely blown down directly. Instead, wind comes in under the canvas, lifting the tent up and pulling out the stakes. When the wind dies down, the poles collapse (falling on the people and equipment inside), and finally the tent falls, trapping the audience under tons of wet canvas. To prevent this, tents were sometimes double-staked in bad weather. Ropes were laced and tied around both stakes (the practice of grapevining mentioned in the earlier quote from Billy Choate). Wooden stakes, though harder than metal to drive into the ground at setup, also have better staying power in windy conditions and were preferred by canvas men on wet or stormy days.[6] In a big storm everyone, sometimes even the audience members, threw their weight on the quarter poles in the tent to keep them on the ground so the canvas wouldn't lift up and then collapse on everyone inside. There are many tales of heroic efforts to keep the poles on the ground, and many lives were saved by such acts.

Loss of equipment was also a serious problem for companies exposed to the weather. A blowdown or near miss almost always resulted in damage to, or loss of, the canvas tent, which was normally torn or shredded by the wind. When the roof falls in, other equipment is destroyed or exposed to the weather. Losses could include wardrobe, scenery, lighting equipment, and sometimes vehicles parked too close to the tent. Such losses usually marked the end of the season for the company—and sometimes the end of the company altogether—because most operated on such a small profit margin. Replacing a tent was expensive and time consuming—even in an era when there were multiple manufacturers and tents were relatively easy to obtain. Each tent was custom built to the specific needs of the company, and each was a different size, weight, and configuration. Such custom orders could not be filled quickly. Replacement of wardrobe and scenery posed similar problems. Not only tent shows lost equipment due to weather. If you were traveling in circle stock or other theatre-based operations, you could lose your gear in floods or storms, with the resulting loss of jobs.

The loss of paying audience members is, of course, another direct result of bad weather. When the storms roll in, people stay home. If you have a run of bad weather, your operation will suffer even if you keep the equipment dry and in one piece. Buffalo Bill had a disastrous season at the World's Industrial and Cotton Exposition in New Orleans, where he claimed it rained for forty-four days straight. It took him two seasons to recover from the financial loss he suffered during this stand.

Another problem for tent-based operations that was caused by cold or rainy weather was carbon monoxide poisoning. This phenomenon came about when tents had double side-walls and a mud flap buried in the dirt to keep early spring drafts out. Stoves, usually little more than pits in the dirt covered by half of an oil drum, called "salamanders" by show folk, were placed in the tent and were usually vented through the tent side-walls. Coke was burned in these stoves. If improperly vented, salamanders consumed the available oxygen in the tent, causing people to develop terrible headaches or to pass out.[7]

Problems with transportation were another major liability for traveling shows. It didn't matter what conveyance was being used—getting from here to there was dangerous, expensive, and time consuming. The further you traveled from familiar territory, the more worrisome such problems became. The hostile landscape seemed more unwelcoming and full of unknown hazards, the chance of friendly encounters seemed less likely, and traveling actors felt more at risk with every passing mile.

In the beginning shows used wagons pulled by horses to move from place to place. Billy Choate describes the difficulty of this mode of travel: "When the roads got muddy, it was extraordinarily difficult to move the wagons, which were loaded to capacity and beyond. At times, the roads became so murky that both teams of horses had to be harnessed to one wagon and pulled two or three miles. Under these conditions, it sometimes took as long as two or three days to get from one town to another."[8]

For much of this country's history, shows traveled by rail. All kinds of specialty equipment were developed to move traveling shows—big and small—over the rails. The basic size and shape of touring paraphernalia was determined by the size of the opening on a standard railcar; the amount of gear you could carry was determined by the price of freight and the allowances given by the railroad companies; the opening and closing of shows was set to match the rail schedule; and show lots and theatre locations were selected based on their proximity to the railroad.[9]

Although railroads provided a fairly reliable and inexpensive way to move a show, train wrecks were common and often deadly. For circuses and Wild West shows the railroads were the only answer to moving large animals, set pieces, mountains of equipment, and large casts from town to town. The biggest shows owned their own rolling stock and paid the railroads to move their cars from location to location. Most of these shows traveled in trains made up of multiple sections. The first section would be loaded as soon as the final audience of the day was in the main tent. Dining tents, sideshows, ticket wagons, and so forth would be loaded and would leave the lot while the show was going on. Once the audience left the lot, the main tent and the show equipment would be loaded on the second section, and finally the cast and crew would board a third section to travel to the new lot. This process was the undoing of many a fine circus and Wild West. Because many tracks were single—in other words trains traveling in opposite directions had to use the same track—schedules were carefully monitored to ensure two trains didn't meet head-on. The problem with multiple-section trains was that switchmen and others often thought the whole train had passed when only the first section had gone through. Once the first section passed, a train going the other direction would be put on the track, meeting the second section of the circus train head-on somewhere down the track.

Less common, but also devastating, were accidents caused when a faster train going in the same direction would catch up with the second or third section of the circus train—causing a rear-end collision. This happened because the switchman would see the first section of the circus train go by hours before the faster second train was put on the track. However, the switchman would somehow miss the second section of the circus train going through. Therefore, the faster second train, which could never catch the first section, would run down the second section and hit it from behind.

Other problems involving ignored signals, collapsing trestles, and damaged equipment were deadly as well.[10] The most devastating circus train accident in history occurred on June 22, 1918, in Ivanhoe, Indiana. The second section of the Hagenbeck Wallace show was stopped because of a problem with one of the cars. The rail line was protected by signal lights, and it was a clear night with good visibility; so this seemed a routine problem, somewhat akin to a flat tire. However, an empty troop train ignored the blocking signal, the frantic efforts of a signalman with his lantern, and a fuse thrown into the cab of the oncoming locomotive by the signalman. Twenty-one steel Pullman cars plowed full speed into the back of the circus train—made up mostly of wooden cars—and the wreckage immediately caught fire. When it was all over

68 circus performers and roustabouts were dead, and 130 were listed as injured. The loss of equipment and circus animals was also extensive but is rarely discussed in accounts of this terrible accident.[11]

Annie Oakley was badly injured in a train wreck while traveling through North Carolina with Buffalo Bill's Wild West in 1901. She was traveling in the second section, which met an oncoming freight train. Although no performers lost their lives, 110 horses were killed. Annie suffered extreme internal injuries and never performed with the show again. There is an apparently unstoppable but clearly apocryphal story that her hair turned snow-white overnight after this accident.

Escaped animals were a problem in such accidents. The circus personnel who were able always made the recapture of the animals their primary focus because local inhabitants tended to shoot first and ask questions later. Of particular concern to citizens were the lions and tigers, which seemed to survive these accidents better than the horses and camels. (This is probably due to the extra cages used for the big cats and the way the cages were secured in the freight cars.) Snakes and other lizards usually fared well for the same reason. After an 1893 wreck of a circus train in Tyrone, Pennsylvania, a tiger attacked a milk cow and was shot by the farmer. A footnote appears in the description of this accident:

> This wreck duplicated in some respects one at Paint Lick, Kentucky, on September 24, 1882. The first of three sections of the Sells Brothers Circus train broke away on a grade and the last twelve of its 15 cars were derailed, three persons being killed. A tiger escaped and everyone was afraid to approach him, but when his cage was placed nearby with the door open, he crept back in. This wreck was due to carelessness of the circus people, who had removed a number of brake handles in order to facilitate the loading of the train.[12]

Not all animal problems resulted from train wrecks. Buffalo Bill had a famous bison bull named Old Monarch that loved to stampede through gardens and other special areas while being moved from the train to the show lot. He became so famous for his shenanigans that he was finally moved in a special wagon to avoid making the community angry before the show even began. Billy Choate tells the story of an elephant that traveled briefly with his tent rep show, helping to set the poles. One night something upset the elephant, and after he disrupted the lot and nearly turned over a truck, he crashed through a fence and disappeared into the night. Searchers finally found him in the woods eleven miles from the lot. According to Billy the elephant was pleased to be found and was no more trouble to the show.[13] Such "disasters" were almost always covered by the local press, and sometimes these articles contain interesting and useful information about circus practices or the performers with the show.

Using trains for travel caused another interesting theatre practice to develop—"red-lighting." The term refers to the practice of firing personnel in the most complete and undignified way possible. An unwanted member of the cast or crew was simply thrown off the back of the train. When the undesirable looked up, all she or he could see was the red lights on the caboose disappearing into the distance.

Another popular mode of transportation in the South was the steamboat or, in earlier times, the flatboat. Steamboats allowed troupes to move upstream and down on the river, and soon companies were not only traveling from town to town on the boats, but boats became theatres as well as conveyances. These boats suffered many hazards from sandbars to boiler explosions, but most lasted a very long time before being decommissioned. As my research on this topic of traveling disasters expands, I'm sure I will find many examples of boating accidents. I will include only one here—the sinking of the boat carrying Buffalo Bill's Wild West to the World's Fair in New Orleans. There are several versions of this accident, and I spent many hours trying to sort out what actually happened. The work I did gave me great insight into the working relationship between Buffalo Bill and Nate Salsbury, his business manager. Salsbury is often given credit for keeping Buffalo Bill on the straight and narrow path of good business practice, and Cody is often described as a poor businessman. My research into this boating accident helped me build the case that Cody was good at his business and that Salsbury had reason to have people think otherwise. Further information like this might eventually change a part of the Cody myth.

It is clear that Pony Bob Haslam, a good friend of Cody from his scouting days, was serving as advance agent for the show. Haslam hired a boat to move the show down the Mississippi to the World's Industrial and Cotton Exposition. Salsbury, who was in Denver at the time of the accident, described the event in notes he made much later:

> The immediate cause of all our trouble was the lack of foresight in hiring the boat. She was a "tub" of the tubbiest description, but our talented Bob was more familiar with the merits of a bronco than he was with boats in general, and this one in particular. When our tub reached a place called Rodney she collided with a boat coming up the river, and was so badly damaged that the Captain ran her ashore, where she was patched up, and

then she set out again on her journey. She moved out into the stream and went down in thirty feet of water in four minutes.[14]

Various local newspapers describe the collision of two well-known steamboats (calling into question Salsbury's description of a tub—and his assessment that Haslam made a poor choice of transportation). All newspaper accounts say the boat went down in only eight feet of water, and all passengers and stock were unharmed (again Salsbury's account seems overly dramatic and perhaps untrue). Another version of the story reports an exchange of telegrams between Cody and Salsbury: "Outfit at bottom of river. What do you advise?" (This from Cody.) "Go to New Orleans, reorganize, and open on your date." (This reply from Salsbury.) Salsbury told this story on several occasions, but there is no proof this exchange ever took place. Cody did travel from New Orleans to the site of the accident, after receiving a telegram from his business agent that everything was under control. This telegram survives, suggesting that Salsbury was determined to put forward stories that showed Cody's business sense in a bad light.

Whatever the truth about the depth of the river and the loss of equipment and animals, the show did open in New Orleans on time—only to be rained on for forty-four days straight. At the end of the ordeal Cody was sixty thousand dollars in the red—a huge sum in 1884. But during those rainy days Cody recruited his biggest star attraction—Annie Oakley. So bad luck, bad weather, and good business sense came together to help assure the show would eventually rise to national and international prominence.

Those who did not travel with their own theatre had another set of worries. If you were relying on the theatre building and theatre manager in each town, you were likely to have uneven success. You might arrive and find no theatre at all (because of fire, storm, or bad management), another company already in possession of the theatre, a town made hostile to theatre companies by the actions of an unscrupulous manager or a company that preceded you, a space too big or too small for your scenery, a set of house scenery too badly painted to be believed, a town racked by disease or other disaster, a theatre building that was decrepit or dangerous for some other reason, or a manager who did not pay for your services. Even when all this went well, every company was at risk of the greatest disaster of all—a theatre fire.

The use of open flame in the lighting of theatres and scenery, and the flammable nature of the materials used in both buildings and scenery, caused many theatres to burn to the ground. Recent accidents in nightclubs remind us of the horror of such fires, and modern theatres are designed with fire safety well in mind. Many of the innovations that keep us safe today were developed in the age of gas lighting. In the nineteenth century fire was a constant threat to touring companies—in theatres, in tents, and nearly everywhere else as well.

Sol Smith includes an extended tale in *Theatrical Management in the West and South for Thirty Years* that reveals a lot about how such dangers were feared by audiences and how managers dealt with such fears. Here is a somewhat edited version of his story:

The cry of "Fire!" in a theatre is a most alarming sound. It is alarming any where, but in a theatre particularly so.

Among the expedients resorted to during the somewhat protracted season at the seat of government of Alabama, to draw audiences to our little theatre, was the production of the pantomime of *Don Juan, or The Libertine Destroyed*, with all the "accessories" of snakes spitting flames, fiends with torches, red fire and blue blazes in the last scene.

Everything went well until the "last scene of all." "Everybody for the last scene!" was called out in the greenroom; when suddenly an alarm of fire was heard in the front of the house! Confusion followed, of course; the auditors tumbled over each other, all pushing for the openings, and I am happy to say that all but one got safely out. I will tell you presently about that one; but first it is proper to explain the cause of the alarm, for this time it had a cause, which was nothing more nor less than the burning of one of the wood wings, the fire having communicated from one of the pots of blue fire, the ingredients of which had not been properly apportioned. In the hottest of the rumpus, a man named Somerville cut his way through the curtain, and in endeavoring to stamp out the burning piece of scenery, the pot of blue fire being unseen by him, he put his foot in it, and the lower part of his leg was very badly burned. He was confined to his room for several weeks.

Next day after the fire—or the alarm of fire—the town rung with an account of the danger encountered by the audience the night previous. The whole affair was greatly exaggerated. The bigoted portion of the Tuscaloosans seized upon the circumstance, and held it up as a warning to all playgoers, and, shaking their heads ominously, said they knew all along that no good could possibly come from encouraging profane stage-plays in a Christian community.

I must here state that, the instant the fire had been extinguished and the house cleared of the alarmed public, I called the scene-painter, and told him I would give him a week's salary if he would produce a wood wing the next morning exactly similar to the one burned. This he undertook to do, and accomplished.

My plan was this: I must convince the people that there had been no fire—that what they had seen was only an imitation!

Collecting together a committee of respectable citizens, we all took a drink and preceded [*sic*] to the theatre.

Here I called the carpenter, and asked him to place the first wood wing in its appropriate groove. This he did almost instantly.

"There, gentlemen," I said, pointing to the newly-painted piece of scenery triumphantly, "I believe you will recognize that; you have seen it often enough."

A close examination now took place, the result of which was the firm belief that it was the same wing they had supposed to be destroyed by fire. The committee of citizens unanimously agreed that the imitation of fire the night previous had been most perfect, and gave me a certificate, which I published in an extra poster, that they had investigated the whole subject, and had come to the conclusion that there had been a False Alarm of fire in the theatre, and there was no danger whatever in visiting that admirably conducted establishment. *Don Juan* had a "run," and was the most successful piece of the season—the last scene being particularly applauded for its truthful representation of the infernal regions.[15]

Although this disaster was minor (except perhaps for Mr. Somerville), the telling of the tale preserved a gold mine of information about the theatrical practices of the day, the response of the town to events in the theatre, and the need for the manager to allay the fears of his audience.

The horrible reports of theatre tragedies (the Brooklyn Theatre fire of 1876, the Iroquois Theatre fire in Chicago in 1903) slowly disappeared as electric lighting and new innovations in theatre safety became standard across the nation. Theatre impresario Steele Mackay took the lead in making theatres safer and more comfortable for audiences. As early as 1882 he had published an article in the *North American Review*, outlining the theatre manager's responsibilities for the safety of the theatre and its public. The article included a ten-point prescription for safer theatres. Some of the things he suggested were to separate the scene shop from the theatre, install automatic trapdoors in the roof of the stage house, hang an automatic fire-proof curtain, teach the actors and crew fire-fighting procedures, provide folding seats to clear the aisles, and provide enough exits for the size of the audience.[16]

Although theatre fires became less common over time, tent fires continued to be feared, and with good reason. Billy Choate describes the loss of a tent to fire in 1942. Taking advantage of good weather, the company decided it was time to waterproof the tent before storing it away for the winter. Before the advent of commercial waterproofing chemicals, companies used a mixture of melted paraffin and gasoline, which was spread on the canvas with sprinklers while it was still hot. I can't think of a more flammable mixture. Through some accident the tent caught fire during this process, and the company was lucky to save the equipment trucks parked nearby.[17]

The end of the tent era of the great American circuses was brought about by a tragic tent fire. Early in the July 6, 1944, matinee performance of the Greatest Show on Earth in Hartford, Connecticut, the tent caught fire and within ten minutes it had collapsed, still blazing. Six thousand people were in the tent when the fire started, 168 of whom perished that day. Many of the dead were children. The loss of circus animals was very high as well. After this accident the Ringling Bros. and Barnum & Bailey circus never traveled under canvas again.[18]

Because touring theatre has been a part of the fabric of American life since colonial times and probably before, the study of these troupes and their relationship with their audiences is a rich and rewarding activity. Focusing on the reporting of disasters—weather, accident, and fire—helps close the gap between the show and the crowd, the community and the company, the theatre and society. The stories of "dragons" are interesting and compelling—whether the dragon or the actors prevail—and the new maps of old territory are more detailed, more complete, and more accurate for the journey down newly discovered roads, rivers, and rails.

Notes

1. Odai Johnson, "The Leeward Islands Company," *Theatre Survey* 44, no. 1 (May 2003): 29–42.

2. Billy (Toby) Choate, *Born in a Trunk: Just Outside the Center Door Fancy* (Kearney, NE: Morris Publishing, 1994), 13–14.

3. Harry Webb, "Remembrances of the Buffalo Bill Wild West Show," recorded by Harry Webb, Sep. 1982, private collection, two ninety-minute cassettes.

4. Choate, *Born in a Trunk*, 164.

5. Ibid., 166.

6. Tom Ogden, *Two Hundred Years of the American Circus* (New York: Facts on File, 1993), 90.

7. Clifford Ashby and Suzanne DePauw May, *Trouping through Texas: Harvey Sadler and His Tent Show* (Bowling Green: Bowling Green University Popular Press, 1982), 45.

8. Choate, *Born in a Trunk*, 16–17.

9. There are several excellent references for the logistics of moving shows by rail. One of the best is *The Circus Moves by Rail*, by Tom Parkinson and Charles Philip "Chappie" Fox (Boulder, CO: Pruett Publishing, 1978). There

is an excellent description of the use of rail for travel by small companies in William L. Slout's *Theatre in a Tent* (Bowling Green, OH: Bowling Green University Popular Press, 1972).

10. Such accidents were so common in the late nineteenth century and early twentieth that an entire book has been written to describe the carnage. See Robert B. Shaw, *A History of Railroad Accidents, Safety Precautions and Operating Practices* (Binghamton, NY: Vail-Ballou Press, 1978).

11. Ibid., 245.

12. Ibid., 368.

13. Choate, *Born in a Trunk*, 43.

14. Nate Salsbury, "Notes," MS, Salsbury Collection, Denver Public Library, Denver, CO.

15. Sol Smith, *Theatrical Management in the West and South for Thirty Years* (New York: Harper and Brothers, 1868), 61–62.

16. Steele MacKaye, "Safety in Theatres," *North American Review*, Nov. 1882, 469–70.

17. Choate, *Born in a Trunk*, 58.

18. Ogden, *Two Hundred Years of the American Circus*, 152–53.

The Circus—Entertainment

for the Masses

Development and Resourcefulness

LaVahn Hoh

O N AUGUST 14, 1944, AT 4:30 A.M. I was awakened by my mother to see the trains of the Ringling Bros. and Barnum & Bailey Circus arriving in town for a one-day stand. The day was cold and gloomy with fog rising off the Fox River, shrouding the railroad tracks in a cloudlike atmosphere. Within moments of our arrival we could hear a train whistle in the distance announcing the first of four circus trains. Thirty minutes after the first train pulled in, the train cars were spotted in the rail yard, and the unloading process had begun. As the cars were unloaded, the wagons were hitched to horses, tractors, or "Caterpillars" to begin their journeys to the circus lot two miles away to be placed, or "spotted," in the precise location on the lot.

As the mists of this cold morning started to lift, wagons and roustabouts arrived on the lot and, with military precision, began their appointed tasks. An article in *McClure's Magazine* likened the appearance of the circus lot to that of a military encampment:

> By the time the menagerie tent is erected, the field has taken on the appearance of a military encampment. Stake wagons, pole-wagons, canvaswagons, each drawn by six horses, have ranged themselves in their proper places. The baggage-wagons and the property-wagons have stopped near the dressing rooms; the wagons carrying the wild beasts' cages are drawn up near the menagerie tent. The horses, both those for humble draught and those for brilliant service in the ring, have been ranged along in lines near their respective tents.[1]

By one o'clock in the afternoon the lot was filling with thousands of us *towners* (a term given to the locals who attended the circus) lining up at the ticket wagons or crowding up to the "bally" platform outside the sideshow to hear the *spieler* (or *grinder*) lure the crowd to "Step Right Up!" and see the attractions advertised on the banner line and witness a sample of the attractions inside. After working through the crowds, we passed through the marquee leading to the menagerie tent, where we were treated to a sight that would evoke biblical images of Noah's Ark. The tent was filled with animals from all parts of the world—elephants side-by-side in a line reaching halfway around the tent, horses, giraffes, llamas, and two rows of animal cages filled with monkeys, bears, tigers, and lions down the middle of the tent.

Leaving the menagerie, we passed through the connection entering the big top. The size of the big top was overwhelming. A cathedral of canvas, poles, ropes, cables, seating surrounding the entire perimeter for ten thousand people and performance spaces to entertain you no matter where you sat. It was the most breathtaking sight I had ever experienced! Surely God lives and travels in an edifice this large and this magnificent!

The afternoon show ended at four o'clock, giving the performers and roustabouts time to eat and relax before the eight o'clock evening performance. Even before the ringmaster's whistle sounded the beginning of the performance, workers descended on the tented city surrounding the big top to begin the teardown and loading of the trains. The loading of the trains is as precise as the setting up of the canvas city on a twelve-acre plot of land. Each wagon has to fit on a flat car to be positioned for easy unloading at the next town. The June 1895 issue of *McClure's Magazine* describes this seemingly impossible task:

> It is a kingdom on wheels, a city that folds itself up like an umbrella. Quietly and swiftly every night it does the work of Aladdin's lamp, picking up in its magician's arms theatre, hotel, schoolroom, barracks, home, whisking them all miles away, and setting them down before sunrise in a new place, and this with such accurate care for the smallest detail that there seems to have been no change at all. No army knows such severe discipline as the troop of the circus train, for its seven hundred soldiers go into battle every morning as a matter of course, and make forced marches every night. Every twenty-four hours it solves a military problem that would have staggered Napoleon himself.[2]

By midnight, or earlier, the first section of the train, with the cookhouse and other equipment necessary to set up the lot in the next town, was ready to pull out. By one o'clock, when the last of the hundreds of wagons and cages were loaded, the circus had completed its work and stay in another American town, giving us memories that would last a lifetime: the noise, the smells, and all the color—magnificent and beautiful—the frights and delights that were and still are the circus.

Since I had that early introduction to the world of the circus at the age of four, I have been fascinated and mesmerized by the development, logistics, and people that helped to shape and direct the American circus, bringing it to where it is today. Though historians have traced the origins of the modern circus to late-eighteenth-century England, there are many gaps in the recorded history of the development of the circus in America. In the past, articles and books written on the subject were not researched carefully, giving the reader erroneous information that has been rewritten in other articles and books and passed on as fact. One very popular book on the history of the circus attributes the origins of today's circus to the Roman Empire. It is understandable that many historians have had difficulty tracing the history of the American circus because many of the records have been destroyed, circus owners did not keep good records, and many of the owners had a tendency to "exaggerate" their shows. The transient nature of the eighteenth- and nineteenth-century circus also makes it a difficult topic to study. The performers and animals would stay in a community (performing in semipermanent structures) only as long as there was sufficient audience. As a result of their relatively short stay, they left little opportunity for critical reflection or study of performances. The towners knew nothing of circus people, their travels, and their hardships—nor did they care. They attended the circus as a break from a very difficult lifestyle devoid of exotic entertainment, wanting to see those skills that were advertised prior to the arrival of these performing groups. Circus historian Stuart Thayer compares it to a sports event: "The variety came in the skill with which the various pieces were presented. The public knew what they were going to see; what they did not know was how well it would be accomplished. Like watching a baseball game."[3]

My research of the circus's early years and its place in American history led me to books and articles by circus historians who expose, through their careful research, many of the myths underlying the development of this cultural form of entertainment. Authors such as Thayer, Dahlinger, Fox, Parkinson, Davis, and Slout have spent many years scrutinizing newspapers, route books, journals, and programs. Their research indicates that the American circus played a very important role in the development of America and expanded with the growth of the nation. The circus was entrepreneurial, industrious, and just as inventive as the citizens that were developing this country.

In the early days of the American circus, performers operated their own shows, but as this new enterprise became financially successful, businessmen took over. Farmers in the region of Somers, New York, quickly realized that they could become wealthy by combining the two most popular traveling attractions of the day: the menagerie and the circus. Mobility led to unique characteristics in both the performance elements and cultural impact of the American circus. For example, street parades, intended as a form of advertisement, became a new, mobile art form intended to depict circus attractions through elements such as the elaborate carvings and paintings of the parade wagons. In turn, the annual visit of the circus became a holiday, transforming the town and its people for a few hours or days as it offered something different from the routine of village life. The visit became a ritual for the townspeople and ritualistic for the circus people. In the pre–Civil War period the size of the circus, limited by the logistics of transportation, allowed an interactive relationship between the performers and the audience. The early American circus can be described as a populist art form, as noted by Stuart Thayer: "While the entertainment itself transcended culture and time, the American circus with its unique qualities held up a mirror to the culture. In the age of the common man, the circus became a common man's amusement."[4]

The American circus had its genesis on April 3, 1793, on the corner of Market and Twelfth streets in Philadelphia, where the citizens of Philadelphia witnessed the first performance by Mr. John Bill Ricketts. Ricketts, a rider and former student of Charles Hughes, arrived in Philadelphia from London sometime in 1792 and shortly after his arrival opened a riding school. The *Federal Gazette and Philadelphia Daily Advertiser* gave the following account of Ricketts's arrival: "Mr. Ricketts lately from London respectfully acquaints the public that he has erected at considerable expense a circus, situated at the corner of Market and Twelfth Streets where he proposes instructing Ladies and Gentlemen in the elegant accomplishments of riding. The Circus will be opened on Thursday Next, the 25th October 1792."[5]

The circus that Ricketts finally opened on April 3, 1793, was a roofless arena (the advertisement in the paper stating "Weather Permitting"), and "seating was divided into boxes and pit, though the pit may not have had benches as the boxes did. Capacity was eight hundred spectators."[6] On April 22, 1793, George Washington attended a performance at Ricketts' Circus. The day after the performance, the following editorial appeared in *Dunlap's American Daily Advertiser*:

Yesterday afternoon, Mr Ricketts Circus in Market Street near the arsenal was opened with his first public exhibition. The Circus was filled with upwards of seven hundred spectators and had there been more room, it is probable that there would have been hundreds more. The debut of Mr. Ricketts before the respectable American assemblage, amongst whom were many excellent judges, seemed very interesting.

His performance was beyond expectation, beautiful, graceful and superb, in the highest extreme; and that none of his attitudes, leaps, or feats, were of a nature to injure the feelings of the most sensitive heart.[7]

Ricketts closed his Philadelphia engagement on July 22, 1793, and moved his company to New York, arriving there on July 26. Prior to his arrival in New York Ricketts had purchased a piece of land near the Government House for the purpose of erecting a circus, where he constructed an open-air arena. The season for Ricketts began August 7, including performances on Wednesdays and Fridays, and lasted until November 4, when Ricketts moved his company to Charleston, South Carolina.

In Charleston, South Carolina; Norfolk and Richmond, Virginia; Baltimore, Maryland; New York City; Boston, Massachusetts; and Providence, Rhode Island, Ricketts repeated the pattern he had established in Philadelphia and New York, erecting, at "considerable expense," open-air arenas at each location.

On October 19, 1795, Ricketts, still performing in semipermanent structures, opened his third season in Philadelphia at the New Amphitheatre on Chestnut Street, where he performed until April 23, 1796. In *Annals of the American Circus, 1793–1829* Stuart Thayer gives a description of Ricketts's new structure:

> The circular building was ninety-seven feet in diameter with eighteen-foot walls supporting a conical roof, which rose to a point fifty feet from the ground. The interior was the usual horseshoe arrangement of the contemporary theatre with a stage at the open end. The ring fence was in the center of the building, the orchestra between the ring and the stage, and the pit surrounding both. The boxes were lower than one would imagine from the height of the walls; perhaps there were dressing rooms under them. Seating capacity was twelve hundred to fourteen hundred and there were stoves for heat.[8]

In the years following his 1795 Philadelphia season, Ricketts continued his habit of moving his circus whenever audiences dwindled, and between 1795 and 1800 his circus occupied "temporary" quarters in Boston, New York, Philadelphia, Montreal, Albany (New York), Baltimore, Annapolis, and various locations on the eastern shore of Maryland. During his 1796 stay in Boston Ricketts shared his audience with a second circus run by Philip Lailson, a native of Sweden. This was the first time in America two circuses performed in the same town at the same time. After twenty-two days Ricketts left Boston and moved his circus to New York City.

In November 1799 Ricketts returned to Philadelphia, where he performed at his amphitheatre until December 17, when "Ricketts' Pantheon . . . burned to the ground, preventing an announced performance of a spectacular pantomime entitled *Don Juan*, which was to have included a scene representing 'the Infernal Regions with a view of the mouth of Hell.' It was difficult to convince many Philadelphians that there was no connection between the fire and the forthcoming production. This disaster left Philadelphia with no circus at all."[9]

On April 3 Ricketts opened what would be his final engagement in America until April 24, 1800. After this final performance Ricketts, with members of his company, left for the West Indies and during his travels was captured by pirates: "Ricketts on way to the West Indies was taken by a French privateer and taken into Gautaloup [*sic*] and there all his effects, horses, and lumber were sold at public venue for the prize money. [But fortunately, a] merchant of Gaudoloup [*sic*] bought all the horses and lumber in for Ricketts [who] erected his circus and in a few nights had paid off his debts and once more stood on his own firm."[10] After a brief stay in the West Indies Ricketts chartered a boat for England and was lost at sea.

Like Ricketts, circuses traveling in the late eighteenth century and the early nineteenth century in America erected temporary wooden performance spaces—many times without a roof—and performed in a city until the city could no longer sustain the show. At the end the circus owner would then either sell the materials or leave the structure and use it again when he returned the next year. After disposing of the structure, the company would move on to another city and build another performance space. Thus, most of the performances given in the first forty years of the institution's American history were in some of the largest cities (New York, Philadelphia, Baltimore, Charleston, Richmond, Norfolk, Albany, Boston).[11]

Following the departure of Ricketts from America, the American circus went into a brief decline, and it was not until 1807 with the arrival of Victor Pepin and Jean Breschard from France that the American circus once again came into prominence. Pepin and Breschard petitioned the Boston Town Council to construct an arena but were turned down because such entertainment was "too frivolous for these sober times."[12] After being turned down in Boston, they traveled to Charlestown, Massachusetts, where they constructed an amphitheatre and performed until

May of 1808. After their stay in Charlestown Pepin and Breschard performed in New York until January 1, 1809.

In October of 1808 Pepin and Breschard were joined by an equestrian
and acrobat named Cayetano Mariotini, who billed himself as "Mr.
Cayetano." One of the unsung personalities in the development of the
American circus, Cayetano was probably the first to move a circus westward on the Ohio River to Cincinnati and Chillicothe, Ohio, and hence
was instrumental in the overall westward movement of the American
circus. Cayetano joined Pepin and Breschard in Charlestown and stayed
with them until the company split in Baltimore in April 1810. After
performing in Massachusetts, New Hampshire, and New York in 1811,
Cayetano once again had his own circus, which opened in Boston on
January 31.

After leaving and rejoining Pepin and Breschard several times during
the next three years, in April of 1814 the three parted ways for good
with Pepin and Breschard returning to Charlestown while Cayetano remained in the West.

Between 1814 and 1817 Cayetano and company performed throughout
the West, traveling from Lexington, Kentucky, to Chillicothe, Ohio;
Cincinnati, Ohio; Louisville, Kentucky; and Natchez, Mississippi. In
April of 1816 Cayetano and company performed in New Orleans. According to Thayer Cayetano's performance in New Orleans was the
longest engagement in American circus history—seven days short of
two years. On September 15, 1817, Cayetano closed his show in New
Orleans because of an epidemic of yellow fever there, which he also
contracted. Cayetano died on November 7, 1817, less than two months
after closing his show in New Orleans.

During the nineteenth century the American circus changed dramatically. What started as a small, intimate show where the audiences were
close to the performers mushroomed into larger tent shows with three
rings and stages between those rings. This development occurred because of the increased interest in the circus, which led to larger tents
and more performing spaces to allow all spectators to view "something."
During the nineteenth century the circus began true touring as opposed
to sporadically moving from one semipermanent arena to another several times per year.

With the crossing of the Appalachian Mountains in 1814, the westward and the southern movement of circus companies began. Thayer
discusses this migration:

> The western cities were growing in 1814. [In] 1810 Pittsburgh . . . [had] a
> population of 4,700, Cincinnati 2,400 and Louisville over one thousand.
> . . . [All] were on the river. Once the showman reached the Ohio he had

access to the whole of the West, . . . and Natchez and New Orleans. Closely inland and easily reached were [cities] such as Lexington and Chillicothe. In the course of 1814 and 1815 and 1816 all these places were touched for the first time by the circus.[13]

In 1825 the number of American circuses was nine. Thayer attributes this rise to "the expansion in population, increase in economy and the large number of American-born performers."[14] But also in 1825 Joshuah Purdy Brown (1802–34) revolutionized the circus business and other traveling shows with the introduction of the canvas tent. The tent made it possible to go anywhere in the new territory, stay as long or short a time as necessary, and perform rain or shine. Tents not only allowed the circuses to perform in more cities, but they also expanded the requirements of moving the show. More wagons were needed to transport the additional equipment; stock (work) horses other than show horses were needed to pull the wagons; and more personnel were needed to erect the tents and drive the wagons. The introduction of the tent also had a profound influence on the owner/manager of the circus. Prior to the tent, the owner/manager only had to deal with a small number of cities in a season; but now they had to deal with 150 or more different towns in a single season, performing six days a week.

After the War of 1812 the population of the country was moving west. With this westward movement the itinerancy of the circus and the use of the tent made it possible to travel in these areas without constructing more permanent performance spaces. Brown's tent allowed him to perform in those larger cities, but more important, he was able to play in the small cities—staying as long as business warranted and then packing up the tent and moving on to another city. With this flexibility Brown could perform and have income six days per week with no downtime between engagements:

In the year Brown first used his new theatre, the leading circus company in the country (of 11) was that of Price & Simpson. This was a partnership between Stephen Price, a lawyer, and Edmond Simpson, an actor. In 1822 they purchased James West's circus company to decrease competition with their dramatic offerings. In 1815 they performed in four cities; Washington (41 days), New York (83 days), Philadelphia, twice (21 days and 95 days) and Baltimore, three times (17 days, 56 days and 26 days). When compared with the average 150 towns visited by a tented circus in an eight month outdoor season, this seems to be a very rigid and restricted schedule.[15]

When Brown and his partner, Lewis Bailey, used the tent in their first season, they traveled from Wilmington, Delaware, into Virginia, stopping at Alexandria, Fredericksburg, Richmond, Norfolk, Lawrenceville, and Lynchburg, and moved up the Shenandoah Valley to Maryland and Pennsylvania before returning to Wilmington. The only location they played indoors was Washington; the remainder of the dates was performed in a tent.

Within five years of Brown's tent the use of the steamboat on western rivers also became so popular that new areas like New Orleans, Louisville, and Cincinnati became prominent circus towns. Thayer notes that "in the period 1834–1860 Cincinnati had the most circus visits of any place in the country, and Louisville was second. Most of their gain in this regard came in the 1850s. J. Purdy Brown's tent gave an impetus for the circus to visit inland cities, to the extent that less than 10 percent of show dates were in the large metropolitan areas by 1850."[16]

Why would any of these shows want to leave the "comfort" of the larger areas of the East? Thayer believes that "the main reason was competition, not just from other circuses, but from all kinds of competition. . . . In addition, the West and the South were more hospitable to their approach."[17]

In 1825, when the Erie Canal was opened, connecting the Hudson River at Albany to the Great Lakes, entrepreneurs and ordinary settlers alike began to flock westward in even greater numbers. By midcentury there were dozens of circuses, small and large, crisscrossing the country, playing wherever new populations justified a performance. By October of 1849 Joseph A. Rowe had already gotten all the way around Cape Horn to San Francisco and Sacramento, where his circus played to gold rush audiences at gold rush prices ($3.00 compared to $.50 in most of the country). In 1847, while touring in Illinois, Iowa, and Wisconsin, Edmund and Jeremiah Mabie—originally from New York—purchased one thousand acres of land in Delavan, Wisconsin, establishing the first permanent winter quarters in the West. By establishing themselves in the West, they could visit places the eastern shows could not reach: "Delavan became the circus center of the West and thrived as such for almost forty years."[18]

As audiences grew, so did tent size. By the late 1800s the tent had increased in size to allow more room for the performance rings—two rings by 1873 and three by 1881. Before long, entirely self-sufficient canvas cities began traveling throughout the country, performing their shows in America's small towns for short periods and then moving on, dismantling their tent cities seemingly overnight.

If the canvas tent allowed circus owners to set up and strike their shows quickly, the second major development that allowed for greater mobility came in the area of transportation, and "it was the railroads that linked together the diverse segments of this vast land so that together they might create the greatest economy the world has known."[19] When John Kennedy spoke these words, it was as if he was speaking about the American circus and the impact the railroads had on it, for the railroad allowed the circus to travel farther and faster and to reach even remote regions of our expanding country.

Advancements in transporting the American circus paralleled those in other industries that depended on nationwide distribution of their products. Before the advent of railroads, the lack of efficient land transportation largely limited U.S. settlement to the "strip" areas adjacent to navigable waterways. Railroads changed this picture quickly and completely. In 1830 there were fewer than thirteen million people in the United States and its western territories. Nearly all of them lived east of the Mississippi River. The sprawl of land that lay beyond the Mississippi was like a locked door.

Wherever railroads were laid, new towns sprang up. Industry and commerce developed. Agricultural production increased and land values multiplied. Representing the best of the American pioneering spirit, railroads laid the foundation for new markets and stimulated unprecedented expansion.

With such advances the nineteenth century progressed toward greater industrialization and the modern era. If speedy and dependable distribution of products was important to the mercantile trades, the combination of the canvas tent with the ever-growing network of railroads moved the American circus closer to modernity as well.

Prior to the use of railroads, circus and menagerie owners traveled their shows up and down the Eastern Seaboard via wagons and boats. The wagon shows—sometimes referred to as "trains"—had many of the components that would eventually become part of the railroad circus. The circus men moved cage wagons and baggage trains filled with the tents and their contents. Some of these shows grew to a size that would rival the later railroad shows; a hundred wagons and hundreds of horses. Some of the early wagon shows included the Spalding and Rogers Circus, the Howes Great London show, the Van Amburgh Menagerie, and the Adam Forepaugh Circus. When the railroad became an option, these shows quickly moved to the new form of transportation, allowing them more flexibility to travel farther and play more cities.

The first record of the movement of the American circus by rail occurred in 1832, when Charles Bacon and Edward Derious moved parts of their show in Georgia. However, it was during the 1850s that circus owners began to look seriously at moving their shows on the rails. In 1851 the Stone and Madigan Circus played the Mississippi valley using the railroad to make many of their moves. In 1853 the Railroad Circus and Crystal Amphitheatre became the first show to tour its entire season on rails; 1854 brought Madigan, Myers, and Barton's Railroad Circus and Amphitheatre and Den Stone's Original Railroad Circus; and 1855 saw the creation of the Great Western Railroad Circus. All of these shows were small in comparison to some of the wagon shows, such as Seth B. Howes's, that still moved "over land."

The early American circus fully realized the potential of the railroad to transport its shows, but the railroad could not always handle the specialized movement of the circus, particularly when there was more than one gauge (the distance between the rails). During the 1850s and 1860s a typical railroad show could be called a "gilly" show—one that transported the show from the train to the lot by manual labor in rented wagons. Equipment for the show would be loaded onto a "gilly" wagon from a railroad boxcar, transported to the lot, and, after the performance, loaded back onto the gilly wagon for transport back to the boxcar. This method may have solved the problem of transporting the circus from the train to the lot, but it was labor intensive and expensive.

In 1857, using knowledge they acquired from previous shows, Gilbert R. Spalding and Charles J. Rogers operated a new show called the Spalding and Rogers Railroad Circus on nine custom-built cars. The tour started in Washington, DC, and traveled through Pennsylvania, New York, Massachusetts, Maine, the British provinces, Michigan, and Ohio, where they boarded Spalding and Rogers's *Floating Palace* (a barge pulled by a tow boat) to continue their tour on the water. Although after this tour Spalding and Rogers did not continue to move by rail, a number of other circuses—Dan Rice, Howes and Robinson, and Lewis Lent among them—followed in their footsteps and used the rails to move their shows.

In the 1860s there were a number of shows that used the "new method" of railroading and the "old method" of moving their shows in the same season. In *The Circus Moves by Rail* Parkinson and Fox state, "Even though the 1860's were showing a rise in railroad shows, playing more and profitable cities, the end of the decade proved to be very difficult for the traveling circuses. Of twenty-eight major circuses that opened, only six completed the [1869] season because of the bad business resulting from endless rains."[20]

Mirroring the aspirations of entrepreneurs in other fields to link the eastern portion of the country with California, circus owners had aspirations to travel coast to coast. The Dan Castello Circus was the first to follow the tracks to California. Although Castello did not move on the rails the entire distance, he used the railroad to reach California by July of 1869. The show opened in Frederick, Maryland, traveling through Maryland, West Virginia, Ohio, Michigan, Wisconsin, Illinois, and Kansas. On January 4, 1869, the show had traveled to New Orleans, where it opened an engagement at the Academy of Music. During the next four weeks Castello toured through Mississippi, Alabama, and Georgia to Savannah, where performances were given on February 8, 9, and 10. The show then began its transcontinental journey. Gradually working their way north as the weather improved, Castello and his partners, James M. Nixon and Egbert C. Howes, laid out a route that would bring them near the new Union Pacific Railway at Omaha.

On May 10 a spike of California gold and one of Nevada silver were driven to connect the Union Pacific and Central Pacific railways at Promontory, Utah. James M. Nixon, Castello's manager, left Omaha on the first through train, going as far as Promontory to survey the possibilities. His report being favorable, the show continued on to Omaha, where exhibitions were given on May 26 and 27. Leaving on the new line, the show visited Grand Island, Nebraska, on the twenty-eighth and North Platte, Nebraska, on the twenty-ninth. On May 30 and 31, at an altitude of six thousand feet, the show played Cheyenne, Wyoming.

> The show then left the railroad and began a four-day march of about eighty-five miles to Denver. . . . June 7, the show drove to Central City, Colorado, reaching an altitude of nine thousand feet. . . . Performances were given in Central City on the ninth, tenth and eleventh.
>
> Pushing on to Georgetown, Colorado, the circus gave two performances on the twelfth, and then began the toilsome trek back to the railroad, pausing in Central City to give two more performances on June 14.
>
> Leaving Cheyenne on the 18th, via the railway, the show exhibited at Laramie on the 19th and at Rawlins on the 20th. Entering Utah, performances were given at Echo City, Provo, Payson, Springville, and American Fork. The week of June 28 was played in Salt Lake City, followed by Ogden and Brigham, Utah. This brought them near Promontory, where just a few weeks after the transcontinental line had been completed. By July 26 the circus had reached San Francisco, where it exhibited through August 21.[21]

During the late 1860s and the early 1870s Americans witnessed an increase in the growth of the American railroad circus and a corresponding increase in touring. With the increase in size of larger urban centers, circus owners realized the necessity of increased revenue to support these large shows traveling by rail. The shows grew exponentially in size with larger audiences requiring larger tents and grand-scale shows to attract these larger audiences. To pay for the increase in materials and labor, the circus not only had to play in cities that could support such an operation, but they also had to move more efficiently, with greater speed and the ability to make longer jumps. Fred Dahlinger Jr. quotes an article from *Clipper's*, making special note of the circuses on the rails in 1872: "'Many of the largest shows during the coming season will travel almost entirely by railroad, chartering for this purpose special trains, and visiting only the larger cities and towns.' Of the 31 shows covered in the *Clipper's* 1872 circus special, eight of them announced their intent to travel all or part of the season by rail."[22]

Intriguingly, touring in the last decades of the nineteenth century was not limited to rail travel. Logically, one would think that the rise of the railroad circuses would have put the overland wagon shows out of business during this period. However, while the railroad shows were playing the larger cities, the smaller cities were left to the overland wagon shows. The smaller wagon shows would play the many smaller cities the railroad shows could not afford to play and also the cities that did not have railroad service.

This might be a good time to correct a common misconception. For some time now, the name of W. C. Coup (1836–95) has been erroneously identified in circus history as the person who put the circus on the rails. The misinformation was supported by Coup, as noted by Dahlinger: "In 1882, a Detroit reporter quoted Coup as saying 'I was the first show-man in this to make use of railroad cars and trains. . . . My show [i.e. the Barnum circus] was the first ever drawn from place to place by special train.'"[23]

We now know that this was not the first venture of moving a circus on the railroad. Coup, however, can be given credit "for being the manager who ushered in a new era in the circus business."[24] To his credit, Coup organized the labor and the equipment to move efficiently from town to town. Coup convinced the railroad to move the trains to arrive on time in order to give three performances.

On April 10, 1871, Barnum, Coup, and Castello opened their new show, P. T. Barnum's Museum, Menagerie, and Circus, under canvas in Brooklyn. The show was the largest overland circus to tour America. During this tour Coup, working with circus agents and the railroads, developed the circus excursion system. Circus agents arranged with the railroads at each town to run special trains into the city the day the show was in town. This tactic proved successful not only for the circus but for the railroad as well, and the 1871 show profited financially, "reportedly earning $450,000 on the $100,000 the partners had invested in the enterprise."[25]

On April 18, 1872, the Barnum show made its debut as a railroad show in New Brunswick, New Jersey, with P. T. Barnum's Great Traveling

Exposition and World's Fair: The Greatest Show on Earth. The show leased "system cars" from the railroads on whose tracks they were routed. The difficulty they encountered was the different size of the system cars. System cars were not designed to haul the specialized circus equipment. In *Sawdust and Spangles* Coup relates an incident in Washington about the problems in loading the train:

> The load out in Washington was problematic. Brake wheels were mounted at the end of the flat cars, which were in the way of loading the cars. The brake wheels prevented the wagons from rolling from car to car; they had to be removed and remounted. The yardmaster refused to remove the brake wheels and insisted that the show be loaded one car at a time. . . . I showed him my contract, wherein the company had agreed to remove all brakes, but he still refused, so I finally resorted to strategy. I invited him to a restaurant, and while we were absent, by a prearranged moment, Baker, the boss canvas-man, wrenched the brakes off, and by the time the yardmaster and I returned the train was almost loaded.[26]

Thereafter, the Barnum show was forced to order railroad cars especially suited to its needs and that would be owned exclusively by the circus.

These first railroad cars were probably a combination of railroad-type vehicles with flanged wheels that were able to ride on the tracks and on the roads. Because the railroad was not fond of building specialty cars, the circus was free to design cars to suit its own needs.

The 1872 show was not the first to transport a circus by rail, nor did it originate the "piggyback" method of moving wheeled vehicles. Two innovations, however, can be attributed to the 1872 Barnum show. First, it was

> the earliest successful attempt to place a complete large overland circus, including all annexes and a parade, on rails and move it daily from date to date. The second achievement of the 1872 Barnum rail show was its purchase of the first conventional railroad cars built for a circus. The Barnum train was the first which was both circus owned and incorporated the stock and flat cars which typified the fully developed railroad circus of the next eighty four years.[27]

The year 1873 was a banner year for the development of the circus with an increase in attendance, an increase in touring, and the expansion of the tent. To accomplish the last, a second ring was added to increase performance space. The second "innovation" of the circus in 1873 was the addition of the "flying squadron." The flying squadron consisted of a group of men who would arrive in town a day ahead of the circus to drive the tent stakes. By having the men arrive early, the circus would save considerable time on circus day in its setup.

Not all technical advancements, however, were positive. In the nineteenth and twentieth centuries circus trains were privately owned, which created financial burdens for circus owners. To move the circus by rail required equipment that needed constant maintenance but generated no income of its own for the show. As a result, between 1872 and 1900 the circus train underwent many changes: "cars were leased and added to equipment already owned by the shows, increasing lengths from twenty-eight feet long to sixty feet long (the longest in show business); while subsequent years saw train length tripling from 1200 feet to over 3600."[28] As the shows improved their transportation, additional innovations were added to the trains, resulting in the configuration of today's touring circus, but the heyday of touring was quickly passing.

The high point was reached in 1911, with thirty-two shows touring the country. During the next eighteen years the American circus had many moments of brilliance, including touring the largest train (Ringling Bros. and Barnum & Bailey toured with ninety-five cars in 1923), constructing tents that held more than ten thousand spectators, and spreading temporary tented cities over land that sometimes exceeded fourteen acres.

But the country was experiencing many changes that would eventually lead to the downfall of many of the touring shows. In 1927 the talking picture debuted, and the last two states of the forty-eight were admitted to the union. In October of 1929 the greatest blow that affected the very crowd the circuses depended on shook the country, the stock market crash. This was followed in the 1930s by the Great Depression. Many circuses folded during this period. By 1933 there were only three railroad circuses traveling in America. Along with the Depression the circuses had to deal with urban growth, streets where parades were no longer practical for the shows, talking pictures, limited land in urban areas to erect their large tents, and movie theatres that were springing up in many cities. All of these developments gave the American population opportunities for entertainment. Americans were learning that the touring circus was not the only form of entertainment on which to spend their hard-earned dollars:

> Like vaudeville, the chain store, the "cheap nickel dump," and the amusement park, the circus helped consolidate a shared national leisure culture at the turn of the century. But in contrast to these mostly urban forms of entertainment, the circus was ubiquitous in all regions of the nation, small

towns and urban centers alike: from New York City to Modesto, California, Wisconsin . . . and on and on. Circus Day disrupted daily life thoroughly, normalized abnormality, and destabilized the familiar right at home, day after day, town after town.[29]

Since its beginnings in 1793 the American circus has endured many hardships, and most recently doomsayers have predicted its imminent demise; yet, like the Phoenix, it has once again risen from the ashes of the 1920s, 1930s, and 1940s to remain America's preeminent touring entertainment enterprise.

Notes

1. *McClure's Magazine,* June 1895, 54–55.

2. Ibid., 58.

3. Stuart Thayer, *Traveling Showmen: The American Circus before the Civil War* (Detroit: Astley and Ricketts, 1997), 98.

4. Ibid., 33.

5. *Federal Gazette and Philadelphia Daily Advertiser,* Oct. 23, 1792.

6. Stuart Thayer, *Annals of the American Circus, Vol. 1, 1793–1829* (Seattle: Dauven and Thayer, 1976), 5.

7. *Dunlap's American Daily Advertiser* (Philadelphia), April 4, 1793.

8. Stuart Thayer, *Annals of the American Circus, Vol. 4, 1793–1860* (Manchester, MI: Rymack Printing, 1976), 10.

9. Glen Hughes, *A History of The American Theatre, 1700–1950* (New York: Samuel French, 1951), 88. For a more complete description of this incident see Sarah Blackstone's article in this volume.

10. Alan S. Downer, ed., *The Memoir of John Durang, American Actor, 1785–1816* (Pittsburgh, PA: University of Pittsburgh Press, 1966), 103.

11. Thayer, *Traveling Showmen,* 1.

12. Thayer, *Annals of the American Circus,* 4:19.

13. Ibid., 34.

14. Ibid., 72.

15. Thayer, *Traveling Showmen,* 25–26.

16. Ibid., 25.

17. Ibid., 26.

18. Thayer, *Annals of the American Circus,* 4:216.

19. "Tomorrow, Arriving by Train," RailFanClub, www.railfanclub.org/remember.asp (accessed Jan. 2, 2005).

20. Tom Parkinson and Charles Philip "Chappie" Fox, *The Circus Moves by Rail* (Boulder, CO: Pruett Publishing, 1978), 4.

21. George Chindahl, *A History of the Circus in America* (Caldwell, ID: Caxton, 1959), 89–92.

22. Fred Dahlinger Jr., "The Development of the Railroad Circus," *Bandwagon* 28, no.1 (Jan.–Feb. 1984): 16.

23. Ibid., 19.

24. Ibid., 17.

25. Ibid., 18.

26. W. C. Coup, *Sawdust and Spangles* (Chicago, IL: Herbert S. Stone, 1901), 66.

27. Dahlinger, "Development of the Railroad Circus," 19.

28. Dahlinger, "The Development of the Railroad Circus." *Bandwagon* 27, no.6 (Nov.–Dec. 1983): 6.

29. Janet M. Davis, *The Circus Age Culture and Society under the American Big Top* (Chapel Hill: University of North Carolina Press, 2002), 14.

Hysterical Historical Fun

The Last of the Old-Time Tent Shows

Dawn Larsen

T HE TENT SHOW IS A largely undocumented, critically un-
assessed theatrical form that was highly popular from the early
twentieth century through the 1950s. With its later addition of a popular character, Toby, the tent show was a major theatrical force that was
responsible for perpetuating rural American theatre. The term *Toby show*
denoted a traveling vaudeville-type melodramatic tent show. The character has been defined by Robert Downing as "a stock character in the
folk theatre of the United States, a bucolic comedy juvenile leading man
in provincial repertory companies of the Mississippi Valley and the Great
Southwest."[1] Although many scholars thought the last traveling tent
company retired from the road in 1963, a few companies struggled, with
the assistance of private and governmental funding, into the 1990s.

One of the last surviving companies was the Rosier Players, formerly
the Henderson Stock Company, from Jackson, Michigan. In 1997 Waunetta
Rosier, Harold Rosier's widow, donated the Rosier Players' complete
tent show to my company, the Hard Corn Players. The equipment includes a 1923-model dramatic end tent that seats 350 people, four 1942
stake trucks, three hundred scripts, costumes, painted drops (some one
hundred years old), and other necessities of the road.

The nature of rural traveling popular entertainment is fleeting. There
is little scholarship concerning this subject, published statistical information is scant, and although remaining troupers are willing to tell their
stories, memories from fifty or more years ago are often inaccurate and
increasingly transitory. Here I will first examine the character of research
on tent shows, then from that perspective report my research concerning the first two owners of the historic equipment collection (Richard

Henderson and Harold Rosier), and finally discuss briefly the values and challenges associated with coupling performance reconstruction with traditional academic research, specifically performance reconstructions by the Hard Corn Players.

My 1991 thesis on the genealogy of Toby shows, "A Continuing History of Toby Shows with an Acknowledgement of the Past and Plans for the Future," made use of a limited collection of published materials and personal interviews conducted with two troupers, Lloyd "Shad" Heller and Ruth "Mollie" Heller. My trip in 1993 to the theatre history conference at the Theatre Museum in Mt. Pleasant, Iowa, attended by many of the remaining troupers, highlighted the speculative nature of both published accounts of the shows and information from personal interviews. I found that much of what I had assumed was fact and used in my thesis was incorrect. Personal memories can contradict those of other performers, and in a theatrical form not generally perceived as worth archival preservation, printed artifacts are scarce and often contain incorrect and contradictory information.

There is some previous scholarship regarding Richard Henderson and Harold Rosier.[2] Having had the advantage of using the Rosiers' letters, personal interviews, and other archival documents from collections at the museum in Mt. Pleasant and the archives at Michigan State University, I can offer corrections to some mistaken dates and other information found in earlier studies. One research issue that I encountered illustrated the suspect nature of conducting primary research about American popular entertainment. The dates and historical information contained in the souvenir programs that were sold at later Rosier performances, 1976 through 1991, were incorrect when compared with Harold Rosier's letters. Waunetta Rosier informed me in a telephone interview that she had tried to correct the errors in the programs but that the director at the college where the collection was being used as a summer theatre program was unconcerned with the errors, believing that they would not be harmful to the audience's experience of the show. The shows were produced at Jackson Community College from 1976 through 1991 in eight-week runs of five shows per week. Obviously, the programs were intended for the performance audience, few of whom were classified as what Erik Cohen has termed "existential tourists," those who demand a realistic and authentic experience of the sort sought out by anthropologists. They were most probably "recreational tourists," likely to cheerfully suspend their disbelief when viewing historical performances.[3] As long as they come away from the performance with a flavor of the historic experience, instead of requiring a purist's authenticity, they are content that they saw a good show, and that seems to be enough for them.

It is also important to report that the character of the audience has changed over the seventeen years that I have either been performing or producing Toby shows. Most patrons that had previously attended historic shows as children have passed on. Generally, my contemporary audiences do not attend the shows to remember nostalgic childhood experiences as their grandparents or parents did. Instead, they come to learn about the entertainments their elderly relatives spoke so enthusiastically about, as well as to be entertained. Therefore, I believe it is imperative to strive to report the most accurate information that I can discover about the Henderson Stock Company and Rosier Players so that future scholars (academic or otherwise) researching these two representative and reputable companies will be provided with credible data.

In my company's mission statement I profess that my company "strives to preserve the tent theatre tradition." I must know, in as much detail as possible, what that history is in order to preserve it. It defeats the purpose to produce plays as a performance methodology for research if the archival and artifactual information that I have to draw from is incorrect or contradictory. Therefore, I must use additional information that I gather from unpublished sources, including letters, interviews, and programs, to provide an accurate picture of the tent-show tradition.

Richard Henderson was the founder of the longest running and, at this date, last of the old-time tent repertory companies. Born in Portland, Michigan, on June 25, 1876, Henderson began a career in acting when he joined the William H. Hartigan theatre company in 1897. According to a 1936 article by Hayden Palmer in the *State Journal*, "Given two parts at four o'clock in the afternoon, he rehearsed them once and played the two roles at a performance the same evening."[4]

Henderson founded the Henderson Stock Company on December 8, 1898, in Otsego, Michigan, with the intention of temporarily employing himself and his out-of-work actor friends. Although touring theatre companies were numerous at that time, Henderson found his business quickly grew to be successful, and he chose to make the company a permanent business endeavor. Harold Rosier asserts in a letter to William Slout: "I remember Dick Henderson telling me that from 1910 to 1920 there were 40 professional stock companies in Michigan alone. . . . He said that nearly every town in the state had an opera house and many companies played the opera houses in the winter and in summer would go under canvas."[5]

The Henderson Stock Company did not regularly perform in tents, choosing to play in opera houses instead.[6] According to an undated and unreferenced fragment of a newspaper article from Waunetta's personal collection, the early Henderson Stock Company traveled by train and played stock in opera houses.[7] Moreover, in a letter to me Waunetta remarked, "Dick didn't like it [playing in a tent]. He didn't like worrying about the weather constantly. Working opera houses was easier. He liked to sleep in the mornings."[8] Richard Henderson insisted on a high level of professionalism, preferring to present what he deemed "legitimate" theatre, not Toby or parody of melodrama, both then popular genres. Although some might conjecture that he used this language as a device to better market his product, research suggests that he strongly believed that the plays he presented were superior, more true to the legitimate theatre tradition than were those of his competitors. A section of a newspaper article in the Mt. Pleasant collection described Henderson and his philosophy of theatre: "Dick Henderson religiously adhered to the legitimate theatre. He was an actor of the old school. . . . And he would never countenance the old drama being made the butt of any jokes. He refused all offers to play in 'The Drunkard,' when that play was picked as prime burlesque of the old school of the theater. He wouldn't be a party to making light of what he considered sacred."[9] Because of his philosophy, his company became known as one of the finest "high-class" repertoire companies in the Midwest. A 1936 Palmer article shows that Henderson's slogan reflected that ideal: "The company produces plays of the better class."[10]

Other reputable showmen touted Dick Henderson as a top-notch actor. Neil Schaffner, for example, "never saw a Broadway actor who . . . measured up to Dick Henderson in *Dr. Jekyll and Mr. Hyde.*"[11] Harold Rosier maintained that Henderson was not only a fine actor but that he was ahead of his time. While most other rep actors were using a very broad melodramatic style, especially for *Dr. Jekyll and Mr. Hyde* (an enormously popular play in its day), Henderson played the eponymous character in a very subtle way. Henderson wore two little dots of black grease paint near the inside corners of his eyes that, while turned away during the transformation, he would smear under his eyes to give them a sinister, sunken look. Along with mussing his hair and striking a menacing posture, according to Harold's story, when Henderson quietly turned and gazed out into the house, the effect was so frightening that people fainted. While this may seem an outrageous claim, perhaps without the contemporary desensitizing visual nature of movies and television, experiencing the transformation through the play for those audiences at that time period might be compared to participating in virtual reality entertainment today. Both experiences could be overwhelming.

Specific archetypal data concerning tent shows are not often preserved, yet they are crucial for the historian conducting primary research
or those attempting to use performance methodology as research. It is
often this kind of information that is most difficult to procure as the
artifacts (show bills, ticket stubs, posters) were disposable. Early Henderson show bills in various collections advertised 10-20-30 shows,
which refers not only to the prices of the seats but also to an entire
genre of theatre.[12] Later show bills reflected higher 25–35–50 cent prices.
Show bills advertised, "Ladies free on Monday nights, if reserved before
6:00 o'clock [sic]," and "Doors open at 7:30. Performance at 8:05." One
show bill advertised, "Pig to be given away Saturday Night!" Most
often, the Henderson season opened in June and closed in November.

Henderson's company was a stock operation, and like most stock companies of that era, it functioned as a collective. According to Waunetta's
April 21, 1998, letter, "The Henderson show always played 'commonwealth.' At the end of the week, the expenses were paid and the remainder was divided among the cast. Harold said one week he got eight
dollars and one week, in the tourist towns in Northern Michigan, he
got eighty dollars." Trouping was difficult, and according to Harold,
"Sometimes they wouldn't do too good in a town, he [Henderson]
would have just enough money to put the trunks and cast on the train
and he would have to walk to the next town."[13]

Henderson retired from the road in 1934. He died at 2:15 p.m. on
Friday, November 15, 1935, of a heart attack. He was survived by his
wife, Fannie, and an aunt, Katherine Henderson. According to Waunetta,
Fannie tried to continue the company as manager but found the road
was too much for her and sold the company to the Rosiers in 1937,
although she traveled with them as an actress until she retired in 1940.

To better understand how Harold Rosier's philosophies compared to
Henderson's, Waunetta provided a quote she thought indicative of
Harold, whose standard remark after viewing most modern performances was, "That would never play in a tent show. . . . They should think
of the families!"[14] Concerned, like Henderson, with the quality of his
productions, though in a more ethical sense, Harold Rosier made his
living in rural traveling theatre for more than sixty years. Rosier was
born November 12, 1912, in Leslie, Michigan. His performance career
actually began by way of the visual arts as many of his paintings were
on display in his father's bakery. A chautauqua artist that was passing
through Leslie recognized Harold's talent and offered to teach him
chalk-talking, a popular chautauqua entertainment.[15] Harold wrote in
his notes: "He showed me how to make my own chalk, what kind of
paper to use and gave me other tips on presenting a chalk talk." Chalk-

talking consisted of telling a story while rapidly drawing a picture with hands and, in Harold's case, feet, that would culminate in a surprise illustration that was often a fundamental symbol representing the moral of the story. Richard Henderson saw Harold perform his chalk-talk act in a school assembly and later in the week as an actor in a Leslie high school play. Thinking Rosier a multitalented performer, Henderson hired him after the play performance on June 10, 1934.

Harold was a versatile actor. The following statement was inscribed in one of his scrapbooks, above a June 25, 1934, show bill featuring his picture: "It wasn't long before I was a featured performer with my picture on their [Henderson's] showbills."[16] According to Waunetta, "[Harold] played comedy, juvenile and heavy leads."[17] However, Harold's granddaughter, Laura Lyn Rosier, quoted in the Lennox paper, maintained that "grandpa stunk as an ingénue, and by the end of that season, he was Toby."[18]

In the Slout letter Harold remembered his days with the Henderson show and discussed why he thought tent rep declined:

> My experience in show bus, was the very last of the old time stock companies. . . . The old shows were dying out then very fast, the "talkies" were cutting in, but perhaps the old shows would have died out anyhow, however I believe the directors and managers were at fault too for not keeping up with the time, managers would fight over territories, stage sets became very old and sloppy . . . but even then I used to make $75.00 a week when the average man would be making $15.00.[19]

Harold played through the 1934 season with Richard Henderson but soon chose to go out on his own as an entertainer.

Waunetta and Harold were married on June 7, 1935. Harold had previously booked a three-day rep for the following summer, the first season for the new Harold Rosier Players. Harold had an idea to rewrite the famous prohibition melodrama *Ten Nights in a Barroom* to include local patrons. He pitched the show to Dr. D. L. McBride of the Michigan Anti-Saloon League, and they toured it from September through November 1935. Additionally, while sponsored by the Michigan Anti-Saloon League, according to a show bill in my collection, Harold chalk-talked, and they performed portions of *The Living Dead*, another popular prohibitionist play.

The next several years provided Harold and Waunetta with valuable performing experience. They continued three- to five-day reps in the summer until 1937, when Harold bought the entire Henderson Stock Company for 350 dollars. The collection consisted of a 1933 REO Speed

Wagon, scenery, scripts, costumes, scrapbooks, props, and sets. The Rosiers asked Fannie Henderson to travel with them since she was a seasoned trouper. She was a member of the troupe from 1937 through 1940. Waunetta notes, "We were young and just getting started. She was a big help to us."[20]

Their territory was the traditional route taken by the Henderson show, one of only seven companies still operating in that territory in the late 1930s. The regular tour ran from June to September and included seventeen to twenty communities. The troupe then played circle stock in the off-season from 1937 through 1939, using Leslie and Mason or Litchfield, Michigan, as their home bases.[21] Leslie and Mason were home bases for a first tour lasting six weeks, and Litchfield was center for a second tour lasting six weeks. The Rosiers worked for several years in theatre and in other private endeavors, taking periodic breaks from the traveling theatre business. In the spring of 1966 the Rosiers bought the Collier Show, an Illinois tent theatre operation, for fifteen hundred dollars and brought the equipment back to Michigan.

The Collier Show had been a variety entertainment company from Farmer City, Illinois, that specialized in three-act plays, vaudeville, magic, and music. Additionally, the show carried a Toby comic but did not produce Toby plays. The Collier collection consisted of a 1941 Chevy pole truck, a 1946 Dodge chair truck, three hundred old blue chairs, ten-foot scenery, props, scripts, and the tent trailer. The show had been stored since 1955. The equipment was in bad repair, and Harold spent all of 1967 repairing the trucks, cutting the ten-foot tall scenery to eight feet, and repainting the chairs.

Rather than traveling like the early tent shows, the Rosiers performed their shows in stationary settings the first few years. The Rosier's first season performing in the tent was in 1968 near Jackson, Michigan, at the Stage Coach Stop at the Irish Hills, a historic tourist attraction near Tecumseh, Michigan. The Rosiers presumed that since they had never traveled with a tent, a stationary season might be a favorable way to learn more about canvas. They stayed for two summer seasons, performing historic rep and Toby shows under canvas, as well as commenting on the historical nature of the shows and characters within the performance.

Deciding in 1974 that they were ready to travel, they booked eight towns near Jackson, Michigan, beginning with Springport. Those towns were on the old Slout circuit, so the audiences were familiar with tent shows and accepted the Rosiers—evidenced by ample ticket sales. They played those same towns until 1975, when Harold suffered a heart attack, which forced him to discontinue traveling and focus instead on the 1976

bicentennial celebrations in surrounding towns. Because the strenuous effort of pitching the tent endangered Harold's health, the troupe performed in community performance spaces, doing slide shows, historical lectures, and a few acts from the tent show until it hired Gerry Blanchard, theatre professor at Jackson Community College, as director during the 1976 season. Waunetta maintained in a June 1998 email, "We played eleven towns, all packed houses." After the 1976 season the Rosiers donated the show to Jackson Community College in Jackson, Michigan, hoping that the college would preserve the equipment, as well as the tent theatre tradition. They retired to Florida that winter only to be contacted the next spring by Blanchard, seeking their help for the summer tent season. They returned to Michigan and Harold taught, directed, and acted for the college in their summer theatre until his death of an aneurysm in the middle of a library show on June 2, 1980. Gerry Blanchard directed the show until 1986. Waunetta and granddaughter Laura Lyn Rosier continued with the show—acting, directing, and operating it until 1991.

My Hard Corn Players, a derivative of the Henderson Stock Company and Rosier Players, using Collier family equipment, directed by a woman who learned the craft from the Heller Toby show, will celebrate in 2005 the 107th birthday of the genesis of an evolved popular entertainment company. I reconstruct Toby shows as a performance methodology for historical research that I can apply to make the shows more engaging to modern rural audiences, a process that perpetuates the Hard Corn Players as a viable theatre business. Each reconstructed performance of a Toby show that I have participated in generated more information, which in turn generated more questions. These questions need answers, thus the need for more performance reconstructions.

Reconstructed performances of any historic form are valuable in two ways. First, performance reconstructions challenge the ways that we think and write about historic performance. Historical reconstruction goes both beyond and hand in hand with written scholarship to provide valid information for the scholar. Historian Robert Sarlos believes that reconstructions and only reconstructions get at the "transitoriness" of a performance. He maintains that although the performance cannot produce an exact replica of the historic event, "it will bring all participants, including spectators, closer to a sensory realization of the style and atmosphere, the physical and emotional dynamics of a bygone era than can mere reading."[22] Sarlos believes performance is a way of knowing and that each participant (audience member, actor, or technician) will learn something more effectively by performing their respective roles than by merely reading about the event.

Second, the information generated can be employed to make future reconstructions more applicable to contemporary audiences. Entertainment value does matter. If we did not care if we entertained the audience, then the audience would not buy future tickets and the reconstruction experiment, whatever result we desired, would be over. Reconstructions can never "recreate" history. Moreover, most popular forms, including tent shows, burlesque, circus, and vaudeville, were forms that continually evolved. As historic audiences' ideologies changed, the successful companies changed to accommodate them. Harold maintained that companies failed if their managers did not change with the times.[23] My reconstructions must be fashioned to take into account the contemporary rural audience and its particular palate while striving to maintain the flavor of the historic performance. What material works now may not have worked then, but it still carries the same "spirit" of the experience. Similarly, what worked then, for example racially biased humor, does not work now, and the historic material must either be omitted or altered. We are very careful in my company to explain that the performance is not an exact replica of a historic tent-show performance. Thus, I attempt to create an exquisite illusion of history built on my informed yet personal readings of history that generate valuable performative experiences for my contemporary rural audiences.

Further, reconstructions of the Toby tent-show genre, as well as other popular entertainment forms, are important specifically because those forms, which have been routinely marginalized and excluded, are forms that represent the common culture. Popular entertainment, from before the time of the Roman circus to contemporary television sitcoms, provides a valid barometer of its culture. Because popular entertainment reflects the culture "at large," it is imperative that scholars attend to it. Toby tent shows represented the ideologies of rural American culture in the twentieth century.

The Hard Corn Players is the only company that I know of in the United States attempting to reconstruct and thus perpetuate Toby shows within the historic tent environment. Most current popular entertainment reflecting rural values comes from this genre. The Toby character and his ideological roots are and were reflected in popular television shows such as, *The Andy Griffith Show*, *The Beverly Hillbillies*, *McCloud*, *Dr. Quinn: Medicine Woman*, and *Northern Exposure*. All contain a Toby-related archetype. Certainly, Andy Griffith was a Toby, smarter than he looks, relying on rural values to defeat crooks and fight off those "wild girls from Mt. Pilot." A further stretch, Ed, on *Northern Exposure*, a simple native of that location who espoused rural traditional values and innocence, could be considered a Toby derivative. Movies such as *Babe*, *Field of Dreams*, and *Titanic* all reflect the idea that the rural folk, with their inherent values, are role models to aspire to. In Tennessee, where we perform, Tobies abound. The Tennessee Pride Sausage company's logo is a red-headed, freckle-faced boy in overalls. Although Toby shows did not invent agrarian values, they certainly reflected and represented them for rural Americans for nearly 140 years. On television and in most movies, reflected in archetypal logos, good still wins through honesty, integrity, and virtue.

My company performs a Toby play I wrote called, "How Now White Cow or You Can Put Your Shoes in the Oven, but That Don't Make Them Biscuits." Although I wrote the plot portion of the script, what we call "plot bits," I incorporated historic sketches found in the Rosier script collection between the plot bits. I modernized the show by integrating, as the historic companies did, regional and local information into the comedy. Additionally, I found it necessary to write the female characters "smarter," to locate them on the same playing field as the male characters, because I am a female actor-manager and because women's roles have changed and are changing, even in the rural South. I reflected the changes by heightening the matriarchal rural family emphasis in plot portions that I wrote to fashion more assertive rural female characters, characters that were considered the heroines of the stories. I found this was in keeping with many of the historic comic sketches found in the Rosier collection.

There are two main challenges I face in successfully perpetuating this tradition through performance reconstruction. First, it is increasingly difficult to keep the historic equipment maintained. The trucks all need new engines, and I store them outside in the weather under tarps because I cannot find a space big enough and cost-effective enough to store them indoors. We have to replace wooden tent poles, canvas sections of the tent, and stage house equipment regularly because of the weather. Federal and state arts granting programs are of little help, as their criteria regard the historic equipment as capital expenses, which neither type of agency funds.

The other challenge involves what I call "teaching new dogs old tricks." Because young theatre students have no contemporary frame of reference for this type of comedy and because the scripts do not read well, it is a challenge to teach this type of comedy. I have found it helpful to show them old Marx Brothers movies, Grand Old Opry comedy videos, and Looney Tunes. I learned to time the comedy like historic actors did: by seeing my mentors perform and then imitating their comedy techniques. This worked well for me because as a young actor I performed my character during a very long season in front of live audiences.

I was able to continually polish my comic technique by trial and error. This is why I continue to play one of the female roles in my Toby play, to give my actors a mentor. However, my student actors only get a five-week rehearsal period to perform five shows. They do not have the time necessary to hone their skills. Returning actors are much better the next year because they have had five nights of experience with a live audience.

It is my ultimate challenge to strive to successfully reconstruct for a modern audience a relevant, thus entertaining, traveling tent-show experience. Coupling traditional academic research methodologies, while striving for greater accuracy of information, with data obtained from performance reconstruction methodology, which seems to evolve and become more valuable every time we reconstruct, provides me further questions to joyfully pursue and my contemporary rural audiences the finest spirit of a particular historical experience, an entertaining participative encounter with history.

Notes

1. Quoted in Phyllis Hartnoll, ed., *The Oxford Companion to the Theatre* (London: Oxford University Press, 1957), 17.

2. See Robert Dean Klassen, "The Tent-Repertoire Theatre: A Rural American Institution" (PhD diss., Michigan State University, 1969); John S. Lennox, "The Rosier Players" (unpublished essay from the Theatre Museum in Mt. Pleasant, Iowa); and William L. Slout, *Theatre in a Tent* (Bowling Green, OH: Bowling Green University Popular Press, 1972).

3. Erik H. Cohen, "Who Is a Tourist? A Conceptual Clarification," *Sociological Review* 22, no. 4 (1974): 547.

4. Hayden R. Palmer, "The Rep Show Travels On," *(Lansing, Michigan) State Journal*, Nov. 29, 1936, 2:2.

5. Harold Rosier to Bill Slout, March 15, 1965, Rosier Papers, Theatre Museum, Mt. Pleasant, Iowa.

6. Opera houses were actually community performance spaces often found on the second or third story of a storefront usually located on the town square. They were given the name "opera house" to lend the establishment respectability, as the term *theatre* was often burdened with immoral or unethical connotations. For more on opera houses see Bruce Speas's chapter in this volume.

7. Stock companies were companies that remained in a town and performed a single play, possibly for a week or two, before changing their bill to another play.

8. Waunetta Rosier Oleferchik to author, April 21, 1998.

9. Undated newspaper clipping, Mt. Pleasant Theater Museum, Mt. Pleasant, Iowa.

10. Palmer, "Rep Show Travels On," 2:2.

11. Neil E. Schaffner, *The Fabulous Toby and Me* (Englewood Cliffs, NJ: Prentice-Hall, 1968), 196.

12. Collections research included the Rosier Players Collection at Michigan State University, Rosier Players Collection at Theatre Museum in Mt. Pleasant, and the collection that came to the author with the Rosier equipment collection.

13. Rosier to Slout, March 15, 1965.

14. Waunetta Rosier Oleferchik in email to the author, June 16, 1998.

15. Chautauqua was a form of intellectual entertainment prevalent from 1826 to 1927.

16. Rosier scrapbooks, Rosier Players Collection, Michigan Traditional Arts Research collection, Michigan State University Museum.

17. Waunetta Rosier Oleferchik, interview by author, April 1998.

18. Quoted in Lennox, "The Rosier Players," 10.

19. Rosier to Slout, March 15, 1965.

20. Waunetta Rosier Oleferchik, "The Rosier Players Past and Present" (unpublished essay in Theatre Museum, Mt. Pleasant, Iowa, 1991), 2.

21. *Circle stock* refers to playing a circle of towns around a home base. A circle stock company would usually perform the same play to the circle of towns one week, then switch to a different play to perform for the same circle of towns for the next week.

22. Robert Sarlos, "Performance Reconstruction: The Vital Link between Past and Future," in *Interpreting the Theatrical Past: Essays in the Historiography of Performance*, ed. Thomas Postlewait and Bruce A. McConachie (Iowa City: University of Iowa Press, 1989), 199.

23. Rosier to Slout, March 15, 1965.

Yankee Consternation in

the Deep South

Worshipping at the *Altars of Steel*

Elizabeth A. Osborne

"THE GREAT QUESTIONS OF THE times will not be decided by speeches and resolutions of majorities, but by blood and iron."[1] Bismarck's volatile and prophetic words are quoted on the title page of *Altars of Steel*, a southern social-labor drama produced by the ambitious but short-lived Federal Theatre Project in 1937. Described by National Director Hallie Flanagan as the Federal Theatre's "most important southern production,"[2] *Altars of Steel* premiered in Atlanta to hot debate, critical acclaim, and sold-out houses—even though its performances ran against auditions for *Gone with the Wind* and the opening of Frank Capra's *Lost Horizon*. In spite of this competition the Atlanta production of *Altars of Steel* quickly became one of the most discussed southern plays of the 1930s. Two major city newspapers, the *Atlanta Constitution* and the *Atlanta Georgian*, ran a series of articles evaluating the merits and deficiencies of the play's political ideas. In turn, *Altars of Steel* was described as "beyond question the most impressive stage offering ever seen in Atlanta . . . as great a play as was ever written," "about as Communistic as a health talk," and "infested with germs of hate and war." Hallie Flanagan describes the play's reception as prophetic: "Audiences crowded the theatre for *Altars of Steel*. They praised the play. They blamed the play. They fought over the play. They wrote to the papers: 'Dangerous propaganda!' . . . Columnists fought over it. Mildred Seydell of the *Atlanta Georgian*, while calling it 'magnificent, gripping, perfectly cast,' found it as 'dangerous as *Uncle Tom's Cabin*.'"[3]

Flanagan's quote begs the question, Was *Altars of Steel* really as "dangerous as *Uncle Tom's Cabin*" to the people of the South? This question is difficult, if not impossible, to ascertain with any degree of finality, but the flurry of debate surrounding the Atlanta production and the suspicious activity revolving around the play's intended Birmingham debut three months earlier denote a play with great potential for social and political upheaval. Indeed, Federal Theatre itself never caught on in the southern region with the intensity seen in New York, Chicago, Los Angeles, Seattle, or any number of smaller cities or towns in these regions, a fact many critics ascribe to both the southern audience's inability to relate to popular Broadway-style productions and the lackluster regional drama available during the period. Yet *Altars of Steel* appears to contradict these criticisms with powerful regional themes, an innovative style of production tailored to the show and its audience, and knowledge of the region that could only be gained by years of life experience. In fact, of all the plays, musicals, circuses, variety shows, and other performances Federal Theatre produced in the southern region, *Altars of Steel* stands out as the one that should have laid a solid foundation for Federal Theatre in the South. Here I will explore the ways in which *Altars of Steel* both reflected and challenged the social, political, and economic hegemony of the South. I propose that those issues that challenged the southern hegemony did, in fact, prevent *Altars of Steel* from laying that foundation for Federal Theatre in the South.

It is curious that in *Arena*, her memoir to the Federal Theatre, Hallie Flanagan discusses *Altars of Steel* only briefly, first touting the media response, then focusing primarily on an innocuous discussion of the monumental set. Jane de Hart Mathews, having written her landmark study of the Federal Theatre Project with substantial assistance from Flanagan, likewise skims over the play. In *The Federal Theatre, 1935–1939*, she refers to it only once in passing: "Although the production of *Altars of Steel* a year earlier by the small Atlanta group had prompted *Variety* to proclaim that the 'spirit of Hallie Flanagan waves over Dixieland,' neither strong theatre nor strong public support had developed in this fast growing metropolis of the New South."[4]

The distinct lack of commentary regarding *Altars of Steel* in the work of Flanagan and Mathews is noteworthy. The Atlanta production created such a stir that newspapers and magazines throughout the country wrote about it. It is uncharacteristic of the politically savvy Flanagan to avoid capitalizing on the proverbial publicity gold mine that the production created both in the struggling South and across the nation. While it is possible that Flanagan simply disliked the production for some reason, it is more likely that the impetus of her response was related to the overall message that *Altars of Steel* conveyed to the city of Birmingham, the southern region, and the country. How, then, did the combination of *Altars of Steel* and the city of Birmingham both promote and contradict the mission of the Federal Theatre Project as a whole?

Inception and Response—The Federal Theatre Contradiction

Many of the difficulties Federal Theatre encountered in the South were due to a fundamental incompatibility between Federal Theatre's stated goal, of producing local dramas relevant to local communities, and the administrative structure of the Federal Theatre, an organization based solidly in New York and Washington, DC. Although this central location was necessary and instigated numerous local successes, both in New York and urban production centers nationally, the structural deficiencies created an intricate web of tensions and disconnects in Federal Theatre communities throughout the country. In the southern region, where Federal Theatre struggled for even grudging acceptance, issues that were little more than nuisances in other regions expanded to become nearly insurmountable obstacles. Memos, wires, and letters from southern administrators to the national center are peppered with frustration related to everything from administrative mix-ups and difficulties with state WPA officials to ever-present complaints over personnel squabbles and lack of talent.[5]

Aside from the typical, yet exacerbated, administrative difficulties present in the South, the greater problem centered on the theatre professionals qualified for relief. According to Flanagan, "We had in the South, due to the fact that for decades it had witnessed no professional theatre activity except an occasional stock company, or third-rate road show, fewer theatre professionals in need than elsewhere."[6] As an alternative to native theatre professionals, Federal Theatre instituted the "flying squadron" method, which allocated directors, designers, actors, and theatre staff to whatever location was in need, regardless of their personal histories or knowledge of the region. This often made it impossible for directors to meet the people of the region, let alone create inspired drama that would reflect their lives. In many cases personnel were brought in from other regions entirely; the director of *Altars of Steel*, for example, was New Yorker Hedley Gordon Graham.[7]

Altars of Steel was written by Thomas Hall-Rogers, a mystery man who appears to have had close ties to the city of Birmingham and the southern steel industry. Several contemporaneous newspaper accounts point to the use of a pseudonym, citing the playwright's fear of violent repercussions to the play and stating that "many believe him to be connected with a steel mill in Birmingham."[8] In her comprehensive chapter on the reception of *Altars of Steel*, Susan Duffy suggests that Thomas Hall-Rogers was, in reality, the Birmingham lawyer and newspaperman John Temple Graves II. Duffy cites the subject matter of Graves's keynote speech before the directors of Federal Theatre's southern region, in which he proposes Federal Theatre attack social issues that speak to the southern condition; specifically, Graves discusses the abject poverty of the tenant farmers and their land, the place of African Americans in southern institutions, and the new political economy dictated by cotton and steel.[9] In addition, Duffy points to the timetable of Graves's proposal and the script submission of *Altars of Steel*, writing that Graves spoke to the southern directors less than six months before the Atlanta production of *Altars of Steel* opened and a mere six weeks prior to the play's first New York script evaluation. Further evidence, though not mentioned by Duffy, places the Birmingham Federal Theatre unit producing a staged reading of *Altars of Steel* for the participants in the conference the very day that Graves spoke when he called for "a play about steel."[10] It was, in fact, in response to Graves's call and the "profound impression [*Altars of Steel* made] on the assembly" of southern officials that the southern branch of the play bureau submitted *Altars of Steel* to the New York office for reading and approval; unfortunately, it did not fare well.[11]

In a letter to Hiram Motherwell, the director of the New York Play Policy Board,[12] play reader and professional playwright John Wexley writes of *Altars of Steel*:

> My most serious criticism of the play is . . . that it is hardly a play. . . . It lacks genuine suspense, contains a minimum of humor, if any, and fails completely to project any convincing characters. . . . I would venture that Federal Theatre audiences would find the play in its present state, very uninteresting and in many places ludicrously unreal, in view of the general, common knowledge of contemporary actualities in the steel industry.[13]

Another play reader, Louis Solomon, commented that *Altars of Steel* showed an "improbable simplification of a complex problem" that was "too naïve to merit consideration."[14] John Rimassa, the final play reader, also rejects the play, writing that it is "Very bad! . . . The conclusion rammed at the audience is: benevolent corporations with assets up to $25,000,000 make for a happy humanity while very large corporations spell disaster for mankind."[15]

It is curious that the unanimous decision to strike *Altars of Steel* from the list of potential Federal Theatre productions was made in New York only a few days before the production opened in Atlanta and months after it was scheduled to open in Birmingham.[16] While it is easy to dismiss this apparent inconsistency in approval and production as symptomatic of a large federal organization plagued by bureaucratic administrative procedures and poor communications, correspondence between Hallie Flanagan, Deputy Director John McGee, and Regional Director

Josef Lentz makes it clear that all three knew and approved of the production, and McGee and Lentz both helped mount the production. A letter dated March 16, 1937, from McGee to Flanagan details the production's process:

> The Atlanta production of *Altars of Steel* will open March 29 and promises to be an exciting production. Gordon Graham is doing a swell job and the production should break all records in the South. [Josef Lentz's] design is particularly startling. Most of the action will take place upon a large cog wheel, width 18 feet in diameter flanked by various other cog wheels of various sizes and heights, all of them moving in relation to each other. The background will consist of rows of huge blast furnaces which fade into the distance in forced perspective, so that there appears to be literally miles of them. Instead of a curtain there will be huge, thick steel doors which roll in and out.[17]

Thomas Hall-Rogers's dynamic sixteen-scene play is set in Birmingham and was intended for the Birmingham Federal Theatre. Initially, it seemed like a match made in Federal Theatre heaven; a play about Birmingham, for Birmingham. *Altars of Steel* went through an extensive workshopping process in Birmingham, received several public readings, and was touted as a shining example of the possibilities of indigenous drama.[18] Early October saw the Birmingham Unit—not the southern regional center of New Orleans—hosting the Southern Conference for the Federal Theatre and performing numerous pieces for the many visiting theatre dignitaries. So in spite of the litany of difficulties from within, the Birmingham Unit appeared poised for breakthroughs with both the national organization and its local audience. On October 27, 1936, Birmingham participated in the national opening of Sinclair Lewis's *It Can't Happen Here*, a production that was recorded as a major success for the Birmingham Project. Although the local reviews are not stellar, they are supportive and encouraging. In addition, the audience survey report completed for the production notes overwhelming public support for the continuation of the project as a community theatre.[19] Yet as 1936 drew to a close, the future of the Birmingham Unit appeared surprisingly uncertain.

In a brief November article in the *Birmingham Post*, Verner Haldene, the director of the Birmingham Unit, tells reporters:

> The Jefferson Theatre, home of Birmingham's Federal Theatre unit, will be dark this week and probably until after Christmas. . . . Waiting on final orders from the regional office, the theatre may take its success, "It Can't Happen Here," on tour through the state. . . . [T]he unit from Tampa may

arrive in Birmingham from Florida successes to take its stand before the local footlights for a stay of a month or more.[20]

The announcement that the theatre would remain dark for at least six weeks is ominous, particularly considering the obviously unplanned alternatives. The unnamed author of this article goes on to note that the Birmingham Federal Theatre will "begin work on *Altars of Steel*, a play of the development of steel in Birmingham, for January production."[21] This January production never materialized. Verner Haldene was quietly transferred to Detroit in early 1937 amid charges of homosexuality, communism, and censorship. The disapproval of city and state officials increased, and when Congress cut the Federal Theatre budget that January, the Birmingham Federal Theatre Unit was shut down altogether; *Altars of Steel* disappeared from the city of Birmingham.

The timing of these events, in conjunction with the silence of prominent Federal Theatre personnel, is suspicious. Though the documented explanation for the physical removal of the play from Birmingham is that the Atlanta Little Theatre Guild invited the Federal Theatre to join a cooperative community unit, the cancellation of a Federal Theatre production for political or social reasons happened more often than one might imagine in a "free, adult, and uncensored" theatre; *The Cradle Will Rock*, *Sing for Your Supper*, and *Ethiopia* are glaring examples of this practice. Is *Altars of Steel* an example of a text so riddled with social and political commentary and revolutionary ideas that it was a legitimate threat to the social, political, and economic order of the Deep South? If so, why would Hallie Flanagan—who had a history of refusing to allow production of politically seditious plays such as this—allow the play to be produced by Federal Theatre, particularly in a region in which the project was already struggling? On the other hand, it is certainly possible that Flanagan and the other Federal Theatre personnel saw *Altars of Steel* as highly relevant indigenous drama for the people of Birmingham, not necessarily as a radical attempt to subvert the southern hegemony. Regardless, it is noteworthy that the troubled rehearsal and production experience of *Altars of Steel* bears a striking similarity to that of Marc Blitzstein's *The Cradle Will Rock*; perhaps the ideology inherent in a labor play revolving around worker rights, unions, the threat of company violence, and ultimately the uprising of a mixed-race working class was so disturbing to the social and economic hegemony of the city that both the play and the Birmingham Federal Theatre Unit needed to be eliminated; it was, quite simply, too relevant to the people of Birmingham.

Social Context—Spellbound in the "Magic City"

Birmingham earned the dubious distinction of being pinpointed by the federal government as "the city in America hardest hit by the depression." Residence of the newly founded southern branch of the Communist Party, Birmingham was home to extreme poverty, starvation, medieval conditions for sharecroppers, and the nation's single largest industrial conflict. Oppression was common, corrupt political and legal systems reinforced lynching and mob rule, and violent terrorism was commonplace. Northerners compared Alabama to the fascist state of Hitler. As Glenn Feldman asserts, Alabama "had the worst record of any state in the country on human and civil liberties and certainly one of the most wretched records in the annals of Western democracy."[22]

Worker organization had all but collapsed during the 1920s throughout Alabama. As Neal R. Pierce explains, "It was a hard society of the survival of the fittest, in which money and power overshadowed all else."[23] U.S. Steel, widely known as "Big Steel," ruled the Birmingham region. As the largest employer in the region, the giant company could alter the city's economy, and with it the daily lives of the people, with a "feudal sway." David Kennedy describes the power relationship in steel towns throughout the country: "Big Steel and the other, so-called Little Steel companies . . . defied labor organizers and federal authorities with impunity."[24] Unions, an obvious threat to employers, were never encouraged by large conglomerates such as U.S. Steel. In the particularly difficult economic period of the Great Depression the efforts of union officials hoping to force employers to accept worker demands was regarded even less kindly.

However, the series of legislation designed to protect worker rights and enacted by Congress between 1933 and 1938 gradually loosened the stranglehold the steel mills had on their workers. Most important was the National Relations Act (also known as the Wagner Act) of 1935, which outlawed many of the traditional methods used by corporations to put down worker protest. In early January 1937, during the period *Altars of Steel* was to have opened in Birmingham, American Federation of Labor president John Lewis and U.S. Steel board chairman Myron Taylor began a series of talks that would end several months later in a surprising agreement between U.S. Steel and labor; the largest steel company in the world agreed to officially recognize the American Federation of Labor as a tool for collective bargaining on behalf of the workers.[25] Prior to this landmark agreement and in the wake of the laws instituted by the federal government, Birmingham enacted the antisedition law (1935); under the guise of rooting out communists and radicals, police and the "red-squad" could raid homes, harass suspected leftists, and would be guaranteed significant protection if violence such as kidnapping, beating, or shooting into a crowd of radicals were to erupt. Naturally, those in the crosshairs of the "red-squad" were often unrelated to the Communist Party.[26]

In addition to the decades of labor strife that plagued Birmingham, the ubiquitous Ku Klux Klan and the pervasive racism associated with that organization, though beginning to fade from prominence, still wielded considerable power in Birmingham during the 1930s. The infamous Scottsboro case (1931) is an example of the power of racism in Alabama during this period. Nine young African American men were arrested and charged with raping two white women. Even though the evidence exonerated the Scottsboro boys, they were indicted and prosecuted within six days; the all-white jury found eight of the boys guilty, and they were sentenced to a mass execution that July. Northern activist groups, including the NAACP and the International Labor Defense Fund, saw the case as an opportunity to make a statement to a national forum. The case quickly rose to monumental stature; it pitted northern Jewish communist lawyers against Alabama's hatred of outside influence (particularly hailing from the North), the KKK, and the perceived desecration of the South's most sacred institution: the sexual violation of a white woman by black men.

The Alabama KKK particularly despised the communist inclinations of the northern lawyers brought in to defend the Scottsboro boys, as communism threatened the racial and economic hegemony of the state by inferring that class (and race) should be leveled in a modern society. The choice of communist recruiters to focus on unionizing African American workers also did little to endear them to the KKK. Communism, and particularly the organization and unionization of the working class, became a focal point for KKK activities in Birmingham. The Klan littered the city with leaflets proclaiming, "Communism will not be tolerated. Ku Klux Klan Rides Again."[27] These intimidation techniques were directed particularly at African American laborers. A typical flyer distributed by the KKK in Birmingham during the 1930s included the following warning:

NEGROES BEWARE
DO NOT ATTEND
COMMUNIST MEETINGS

Paid organizers for the communists are only trying to get negroes in trouble. Alabama is a good place for good negroes to live in, but it

is a bad place for negroes who believe in SOCIAL EQUALITY.
The Ku Klux Klan Is Watching You.
TAKE HEED
Tell the communist leaders to leave. Report all communist meetings
to the
Ku Klux Klan
Post office Box 651, Birmingham, Alabama[28]

Those who attended union rallies were either attacked themselves or saw their family members assaulted. One man's wife was shot because he attended a union meeting. A black man was nailed to his front door by his thumbs for a similar crime. Unions, communism, and racial equality were linked in the minds of Alabama KKK members; they were steps along the road to social and ideological disaster. The struggle for power would continue for nearly a decade; unfortunately, the Federal Theatre production of *Altars of Steel* portrayed the working-class struggle against the dominant hegemony, directly challenging the power of United Steel on social, racial, political, and economic grounds. It is hard to believe that the Birmingham leaders of U.S. Steel would have been blind to this obvious parallel and harder to believe that they would have made no move to preserve the hierarchy of power already in place.[29]

Altars of Steel—Benevolent Southern Gentlemen and Greedy Northern Conglomerates

Altars of Steel dramatizes the story of the local Birmingham steel mill that is bought out by a national company from the North, United Steel. A communist worker, Draper, attempts to incite discontent among the workers; and the new northern conglomerate owner, Karl Jung, alienates the workers by demanding a work speed-up, reducing wages, paying the workers in money that can only be used at the company store, prohibiting worker meetings and unions, and disbanding the safety department. He refuses to upgrade the worn-out equipment and confides in the management team that he plans to replace the old furnaces and machinery only when they break; at that time he plans to drastically reduce the number of workers as well. In stark contrast to the benevolent reign of the previous owner, Mr. Worth, Jung clearly cares for neither the working men nor the community. In spite of repeated warnings by the former management—warnings that become so forceful that the entire team resigns instead of ordering the laborers to continue working on the unsafe hearth—Jung demands increased production. Nineteen workers die brutal deaths in the accident that follows. Urged on by the

The riot scene from *Altars of Steel*. Mr. Worth (center), separated from the men by armed guards, vainly attempts to explain their moral victory over Mr. Jung and United Steel. Federal Theatre Project, Special Collections and Archives, George Mason University Libraries.

communist upstart, the survivors riot and begin tearing the mill apart in their efforts to find and kill Jung. Trapped as he waits for the United Steel strikebreakers to arrive and deserted by the corrupt civil authorities, Jung begs Worth to reason with the men. Worth agrees, on the condition that Jung admits responsibility for the men's deaths and reinstates Worth's company majority. Jung agrees (though later destroys the evidence of his guilt); Worth endeavors to reason with the men but tempers flare, and the communist fires a shot at Worth, killing him. Many die in the ensuing bloodbath, and the play closes with the following announcement reported over a loudspeaker:

> The Special grand jury investigating the tragic death of nineteen men in the fatal explosion of Number Four open hearth at the plant of the United Steel, Iron, and Coal Company has returned a verdict absolving any individual from criminal guilt. The verdict recites that while the men were killed in the firing of a defective furnace, there is no evidence to prove definitely who gave the order to fire the furnace. There are charges and

counter charges of political pressure and bribery to influence the verdict of NOT GUILTY.[30]

On the surface the play appears to simply replay a series of events that actually occurred when Judge Elbert Gary (U.S. Steel's paternalistic chief executive in Birmingham) passed away and new management arrived. As the play depicts, the new management was unconcerned with worker safety, took advantage of the workers, forced a company union on the men, and conspired with local police and government officials to prevent worker organization.[31] During the early years of the Depression steel production in Birmingham reached its all-time low, mills operated at between 40 and 60 percent of capacity, and the blast furnaces that once lit the nighttime sky with a continuous scarlet glow burned only sporadically.[32] While these conditions are certainly reflected in the play, it is also important to note the similarity to the events of 1907. Prior to the financial panic of 1907, Tennessee Coal and Iron (TCI) was one of the major employers in the city of Birmingham, as well as a leading producer of pig iron for the United States. The economic crisis caught TCI in the midst of expansion and associated debt, and the dramatic decrease in product demand left the company financially vulnerable. With Moore and Schley, a New York brokering firm heavily invested in TCI, close to collapse and amid widespread fear of the repercussions of such a failure in the stock market, the executive board of U.S. Steel debated the purchase of TCI. After numerous conferences the board sent an envoy to President Theodore Roosevelt to determine his position regarding the major problem associated with the purchase; the combined interests of U.S. Steel and TCI would constitute 60 percent of the iron and steel market, thereby creating a monopoly.[33] Roosevelt's tacit approval focused on the benevolent gesture proposed by U.S. Steel: "[The representatives of U.S. Steel] feel that it is immensely to their interest, as to the interest of every responsible business man, to try and prevent a panic and general industrial smash up at this time. . . . Of course I could not advise them to take the action proposed [but] I felt it no public duty of mine to interpose any objection." Buoyed by Roosevelt's support, U.S. Steel purchased TCI for approximately one-third of its market value.[34]

U.S. Steel's "munificent" purchase of TCI is replayed in the early scenes of *Altars of Steel* with an almost alarming realism. As the play unfolds, the audience learns that Mr. Worth is heavily in debt. In spite of Worth's extraordinary efforts to pay these debts off, United Steel purchases every bank in the state of Alabama so as to call Worth's loans and foreclose when he is unable to pay. Worth appeals to the federal government: "With the acquisition of this property they will control over sixty percent [of America's steel business, but] the government does not feel called upon to intervene" (4.2–4). In *Altars of Steel* United Steel acquires the Southern Steel Company for one quarter of its value.

While the parallels to the U.S. Steel procurement of TCI in 1907 and United Steel's hostile takeover of the Southern Steel Company in *Altars of Steel* are striking, the play goes on to reflect and challenge the social and cultural hegemony of contemporaneous Birmingham. One of the first scenes of the play introduces the concept of unionization, as well as a communist worker, who immediately sets out to inflame tensions among the other working men:

> BILL: Then stand by the company. That's where you get your pay from. The more money the company makes the more time you'll work.
> 1ST WORKER: Ain't nobody going to talk me into joinin' no union.
> CHECKER: Maybe not—but you ought to hear the talk that passes this window every day. Somebody ought to tell Old Man Worth.
> DRAPER: (*who until now has been in the background*) Turn informer, would you? Don't you know enough to stick by your class?
> (There is a sudden silence)
> BILL: Who the hell are you buddie? (1.4)

This dialogue shows several facets of the southern struggle for power during this period. First, the seasoned working men in the scene feel no need to join a union because their current employer, Mr. Worth, is a reasonable, caring, and genteel man in their eyes. As is revealed in the following scene, when one of the seasoned workers makes known Draper's communist beliefs, Mr. Worth calls Draper to his office to discuss the matter. In the face of Draper's incendiary accusations and refusal to discuss his position rationally, Mr. Worth gives him an advance on his paycheck, allows the man to take both his communist leaflets and his pistol back to work in the mill, and says simply, "He's so young . . . and he's a sick man—sick in his mind" (2.3). Mr. Worth's words not only show his kind practicality but also demonstrate an almost condescending pity for the poor, mentally ill communists that populate the city and cause trouble. He does not take Draper seriously, in spite of his loaded pistol and inflammatory ideas; this treatment effectively robs Draper of his political virility in the eyes of both the working men and the audience. Dennis Jerz, in his analysis of *Altars of Steel*, argues that Draper is "a drifter, a newcomer, . . . a murderer [and a] rhetorically effective agitator, . . . not a sympathetic character."[35] While it is certainly true that Draper, the man who ultimately shoots and kills Mr. Worth, is dangerous, it is vital to realize his role within the context of the social and cultural hegemony. Draper's communistic beliefs in conjunction with his outspoken, irrational, and blasphemous remarks place him in a position in which he is seen as one who capitalizes on the tragic deaths of fellow workers in order to create chaos, not as a leader who will better the situation of the workers.

It is also interesting to note that, although the play makes no mention of the Ku Klux Klan, the men react with a careful vigilance once they learn that he is a communist with an eye toward unionizing. Even Mr. Worth asks his foreman to "keep an eye on Draper" (2.4). Although it is certainly possible that this reaction is due to a distrust of outsiders or anxiety related to unionizing and strikes, it is also possible that this reaction carries an undercurrent of fear with respect to a Klan backlash. The Klan response to communism and unionization was both documented and violent in Birmingham for men and women of all races; serious repercussions, including beatings, attacks on one's family, and even murder, befell those who took part in such affairs during this period. The lack of Klan presence is conspicuous in the play, particularly when one considers that the play was written during a "wave of anti-Communist police repression" that reached its height with the beating of Joseph Gelders, an educated Jewish Birmingham native who became the political liaison for the communist party.[36]

Finally, *Altars of Steel* calls attention to southern pride and nationalism. In the play southerners are characterized by well-mannered, courteous men like Mr. Worth and honorable, hardworking laborers. As long as the steel mill is controlled by Mr. Worth, the men are safe and basically content; it is only when the northern steelworks purchases the company that trouble begins. Their reign ushers in a time of strikes, riots, and murder, a period that is capitalized on by Draper, the communist from the North. Again, Draper is shunned by the workers until the northern management treats them poorly, thereby inciting the ensuing problems. It is also fitting that it is the southerners who suffer at the end of the play. After raising the mob of angry workers to a fever pitch, Draper shoots at Mr. Worth, who has returned from his resignation on the condition that he will regain his power over the mill and reinstate the previous working conditions for the men; Draper's shot kills him, leaving his son to follow in his footsteps.[37] Here the communist murders the beloved southern gentleman while the Yankee industrialists greedily cause nineteen workers to burn to death. The play ends with Jung escaping entirely, the fate of the southern mill uncertain, and the workers in a state of anger and frustration that would make any steel mill owner wish to sneak quietly out of the theatre before anyone realizes his identity. This unsettled and provocative ending leaves one appalled at the outright injustice of the situation, and it is not difficult to imagine the agitated state of mind that would engulf a Birmingham audience. The lesson in the abuse of power ends in a call for the South to rise from the ashes of the steel mill and regain its resources, people, and pride. In this way *Altars of Steel* plays on southern pride, nationalism, and the potential power of the proportionally enormous working class in a way that clearly challenges the social, political, and cultural hegemony of Birmingham.

Conclusion

Vital to the study of the Federal Theatre Project as both national theatre and as a reflection of the constantly evolving relationship between Federal Theatre and its surrounding communities, *Altars of Steel* serves as a case study for that troubled region—the South. The production—and lack of production—of *Altars of Steel* provides fertile ground for the study of Federal Theatre and its ability to inspire indigenous drama that is truly by and about the people of a given region. In this particular case it appears that the production reflected the people of Birmingham so closely that it was deemed dangerous, particularly in light of the contemporaneous issues surrounding U.S. Steel and the American Federation of Labor. In its ability to incite change *Altars of Steel* provides a glimpse into at least a portion of the working-class minds in Birmingham during the tumultuous Great Depression, illustrating the fears of the dominant hegemony and the potential power of the working class in Birmingham, Alabama.

Was *Altars of Steel* as "dangerous as *Uncle Tom's Cabin*" to the hierarchy of power in place in the South? In Birmingham it quite possibly was. Certainly, the play both reflects and challenges the political, social, and economic hegemony prevalent in Birmingham during the Great Depression. A product of a troubled time, *Altars of Steel* follows in the tradition of agitprop plays like *Waiting for Lefty* and *The Cradle Will Rock*. It offers no simple solution, refrains from glossing over tough issues, and forces the audience to contemplate the chaos of the powerless worker. While it may not have led to a riot in Birmingham, it is likely that it would at the very least have provided the impetus for future discussion among the workers. Unfortunately, the Birmingham Federal Theatre Project was a promise left unfulfilled; *Altars of Steel* is evidence that the people of Birmingham were in dire need of an organization that would provide a forum for the issues of the working class. The

Federal Theatre response to the pressures on the Birmingham Unit, and to the play as a whole, is another intriguing question that merits further exploration.

Notes

1. Thomas Hall-Rogers, *Altars of Steel*, Playscripts File, 1936–39, Box 578, Library of Congress Federal Theatre Project Collection.

2. Hallie Flanagan, *Arena* (New York: Duell, Sloan, and Pearce, 1940), 88.

3. Ralph T. Jones, "*Altars of Steel* Highly Praised as Best Drama Ever Presented Here," *Atlanta Constitution*, April 2, 1937, 11; Tarleton Collier, "Behind the Headlines," *Atlanta Georgian*, April 6, 1937, 3; Mildred Seydell, "*Altars of Steel* Aids Communism with Tax Money," *Atlanta Georgian*, April 4, 1937, 4D; Flanagan, *Arena*, 89. For a detailed discussion of the newspaper coverage of *Altars of Steel* in Atlanta see Susan Duffy, *American Labor on Stage: Dramatic Interpretations of the Steel and Textile Industries in the 1930s* (Westport, CT: Greenwood Press, 1996), 96–101; and John Russell Poole, *The Federal Theatre Project in Georgia and Alabama: An Historical Analysis of Government Theatre in the Deep South* (PhD diss., University of Georgia, 1995), 80–88.

4. Jane de Hart Mathews, *The Federal Theatre, 1935–1939: Plays, Relief, and Politics* (Princeton, NJ: Princeton University Press, 1967), 181.

5. The Federal Theatre Project records at the National Archives include numerous examples of this. See National Archives and Records Administration, Works Progress Administration, Federal Theatre Project, Record Group 69 (hereafter NARA, WPA, FTP, RG 69), Entry 850, National Office Correspondence with Regional Offices.

6. Flanagan, *Arena*, 81. While Flanagan's statement could be read as condescending, the context of her comment shows that she is referring only to those workers designated by the WPA as theatre professionals qualified to receive relief. However, this statement does point to a disparity in the understanding of the types of performance that constitute professional theatre, placing legitimate stage drama above regional tent shows, oral traditions, or other forms of performance.

7. Those familiar with the Federal Theatre Project may recall Hedley Gordon Graham as the director of Chicago's 1936 hit review *O'Say Can You Sing*, as well as numerous productions in New York. Following the Atlanta production of *Altars of Steel*, Graham directed the Tampa production of *Altars of Steel*, as well as the Spanish version of *O'Say Can You Sing*.

8. "Problem Play Author's Name Is Kept Secret," *Philadelphia Inquirer*, April 18, 1937.

9. See John McGee, *Federal Theatre of the South: A Supplement to the Federal Theatre National Bulletin* 1, no. 2 (Oct. 1936): n.p., NARA, WPA, FTP, RG 69, Entry 920, Regional Publications Describing Federal Theatre Activities, 1936–39, Box 357.

10. Duffy, *American Labor on Stage*, 83–85.

11. McGee, *Federal Theatre of the South*, n.p.

12. A relatively short-lived board, the Play Policy Board was responsible for play reading and approval on a national basis for the Federal Theatre.

13. John Wexley to Hiram Motherwell, March 27, 1937, "*Altars of Steel*," Playreader Reports File, 1935–39, Box 138, Library of Congress Federal Theatre Project Collection.

14. Louis Solomon, "Playreader Report: *Altars of Steel*," Play Reader Reports File, 1935–39, Box 138, Library of Congress Federal Theatre Project Collection.

15. John Rimassa, "Playreader Report: *Altars of Steel*," Play Reader Reports File, 1935–39, Box 138, Library of Congress Federal Theatre Project Collection.

16. Just as *Altars of Steel* slipped through the numerous rejections of the various play readers, Hallie Flanagan was in the process of instituting a new policy for play approval. During the fall of 1936, buoyed by the promise of WPA administrator Harry Hopkins that he would support any Federal Theatre play that had Flanagan's personal approval, Flanagan insisted that all Federal Theatre production plans must be made at least three months in advance, pass through the Play Policy Board, and then gain Flanagan's approval prior to production. This process was based on the system already in place in Birmingham, in which the Southern Bureau collected regional material of promise and sent the most promising to the national Play Policy Board for approval. Although this procedure was still in the process of being implemented when *Altars of Steel* began rehearsals, it is clear that the intended January production was subject to this system, as is evidenced by Verner Haldene's proposal for the first quarter of 1937, in which he places the opening of *Altars of Steel* in late January. See Mathews, *Federal Theatre, 1935–1939*, 96–97; Poole, *Federal Theatre Project in Georgia and Alabama*, 56–59; Verner Haldene, "Three Month Production Bulletin for Period Beginning January 1, 1937," Dec. 29, 1936, NARA, WPA, FTP, RG 69.

17. John McGee to Hallie Flanagan, memorandum, March 16, 1937, NARA, WPA, FTP, RG 69, E839, General Correspondence with the National Office, Box 25, Southern Trip, 2–3.

18. Poole, *Federal Theatre Project in Georgia and Alabama*, 51.

19. Dana Rush, "Audience Survey Report for *It Can't Happen Here*," Nov. 23, 1936, NARA, WPA, FTP, RG 69, E907, National Play Bureau Audience Survey Reports, Box 254.

20. *Birmingham Post*, "Federal Unit Drops Curtain," Nov. 25, 1936, clipping file, Birmingham Federal Theatre, Birmingham Public Library.

21. Ibid.

22. Feldman, *Politics, Society and the Klan in Alabama* (Tuscaloosa: University of Alabama Press, 1999), 219–20; Robin D. G. Kelley, *Hammer and Hoe: Alabama Communists during the Great Depression* (Chapel Hill: University of North Carolina Press, 1990), 14.

23. Neal R. Pierce, *The Deep South States of America: People, Politics, and Power in the Seven Deep South States* (New York: Norton, 1974), 282.

24. While it may be difficult to believe that a single company could wield so much power, it is important to understand the mammoth amount of money and steel that was produced by U.S. Steel. This company's mills in Pittsburgh, Birmingham, and Chicago produced more steel than all of Germany, the second largest steel-producing country in the world. See David M. Kennedy, *Freedom from Fear: The American People in Depression and War, 1929–1945* (New York: Oxford University Press, 1999), 303.

25. Walter Galenson, *The CIO Challenge to the AFL: A History of the American Labor Movement, 1935–1941* (Cambridge, MA: Harvard University Press, 1960), 92.

26. William Warren Rogers, Robert David Ward, Leah Rawls Atkins, and Wayne Flint, *Alabama: The History of a Deep South State* (Tuscaloosa: University of Alabama Press, 1994), 480–85.

27. Ibid., 274.

28. Quoted in Kelley, *Hammer and Hoe*, 75.

29. Ibid., 223–27.

30. Hall-Rogers, *Altars of Steel*, sc. 16, p. 1. Subsequent references are cited in the text by scene and page number.

31. Rogers et al., *Alabama*, 470. Company unions did not serve the needs of the workers. These organizations were orchestrated by the management as a tool to control the workers from within, while showing the public that the company embraced "worker" organization.

32. Marjorie Longenecker White, *The Birmingham District: An Industrial History and Guide* (Birmingham, AL: Birmingham Historical Society, 1981), 65.

33. This description of the events preceding U.S. Steel's acquisition of TCI is a result of the compilation of several studies. See White, *The Birmingham District*, 91–97; Rogers et al., *Alabama*, 284–86; Kenneth Warren, *Big Steel: The First Century of the United States Steel Corporation, 1901–2001* (Pittsburgh, PA: University of Pittsburgh Press, 2001), 77–83; and Ethel Armes, *The Story of Coal and Iron in Alabama* (Birmingham, AL: Birmingham Chamber of Commerce, 1910).

34. T. R. Roosevelt to Attorney General Bonaparte, Nov. 4, 1907, quoted in *Bulletin of the American Iron and Steel Institute*, Feb. 1, 1909, 1.

35. Dennis G. Jerz, *Technology in American Drama, 1920–1950: Soul and Society in the Age of the Machine* (Westport, CT: Greenwood Press, 2003), 88.

36. Kelley, *Hammer and Hoe*, 130–31.

37. Several versions of the play exist, each of which is structured slightly differently and offers a different ending. In the version on file at the National Archives Mr. Worth's son is killed at the end of the play as his father tries to diffuse the angry mob of workers. The version discussed in this article was produced for Atlanta and Miami audiences.

Caught on the Rails

The Traveling Black Performer as Prey

Barbara Lewis

I N THE OPENING MONOLOGUE OF *The Little Tommy Parker Celebrated Colored Minstrel Show* by Carlyle Brown, an award-winning African American playwright knowledgeable in black performance history, Henry, an African American blackface performer—one of six in the play who are touring the Midwest in a railroad car—recalls shining shoes as a boy outside the Opera House in Philadelphia.[1] He remembers that in the nineteenth century Philadelphia was a major theatrical town, and those who wanted to break into the business watched for their opportunities by staying close to the recognized centers of cultural activity. Inside the theatre a big-name minstrel troupe was headlining and attracting a crowd, which gave Henry steady customers, as well as a taste for the excitement and the kind of money to be had giving people pleasure in the world of the theatre. The first image conjured up in the play is one of opposition, inside versus outside. In *Tommy Parker*, written at the end of the twentieth century and first presented at Penumbra in Minneapolis and later at the Negro Ensemble Company in 1990, as well as subsequently in Denver and Kansas City, Brown sets an incident of racial opposition against the backdrop of blackface performance at the end of the nineteenth century, when African Americans were entering the field of entertainment in large numbers.

Minstrelsy was the keyhole through which African Americans had to squeeze and contort themselves in order to gain access in greater numbers to the official stage that offered self-representation and even celebrity to the fortunate few. Wearing layers of bright, traffic-stopping crimson on their lips and blackened burnt cork on their faces, exaggerating the starkness of their difference to the point of grotesqueness, was the convention they inherited from Anglo minstrel performers. Those who, like Henry, had a sincere love for the stage accepted these givens and worked to change them from the inside—elbowing increased room for themselves—to better accommodate their psychological and social needs. After the Civil War, black men, legally free, portrayed themselves in popular venues with greater frequency, but they did so underneath the weight and burden of masks and stereotypes that Anglo minstrel performers had made fashionable and canonical. In public representation their bodies were theirs again, but only provisionally. Further, following Reconstruction, the practice of lynching escalated and changed character to the point where the public dismantling of the black body became a collective pastime. For African Americans, finding a way to insert their whole selves into the public sphere was a challenge. For many black performers the theatre was not simply a matter of bringing their talent to the marketplace at a good price. To be involved in theatre was also political. According to Frederick Douglass, the most well-known African American activist and thinker of the nineteenth century, minstrelsy was "a site of political struggle for representation."[2]

Beginning early and lasting throughout the span of the nineteenth century, minstrelsy reigned supreme on American stages and was internationally popular, influencing performance patterns as far away as Australia, Ghana, India, and South Africa. It first riveted public imagination in the Jacksonian era, when Anglo males—especially Daddy "Jim Crow" Rice, the Elvis Presley and Eminem of his day—displayed themselves as dancing, joking, and singing counterfeit black males (as well as, on occasion, black females), splitting the enslaved body from its skin and its personhood, thus evacuating, symbolically, the representative black self from the public sphere. The minstrel sway was long lasting, persisting in film, amateur theatricals, and television into the twentieth century. Al Jolson blacked up. So did Bing Crosby, the Marx Brothers, Fred Astaire, Judy Garland, and Doris Day, among others.[3] In *Bamboozled* (2001) Spike Lee acknowledged the endurance of this performance phenomenon, arguing that its appeal is still a visual crowd pleaser. According to cultural critic W. T. Lhamon Jr., minstrelsy, which went underground for a while with its proponents affecting the gesture and sound of inner city populations, has its contemporary children: "The post–World War II era of rock 'n' roll and the populist core of postmodernism . . . are all, at least in part, heirs of blackface performance."[4] Minstrelsy continues to have significance and relevance in the twenty-first century.

In *Tommy Parker* Brown highlights the dilemma that the African American performer faced as the rule of slavery gave way to the law of

segregation in a crucial and formative period at the end of the nineteenth century. There was a break in regimes, an aperture. One organi-
zational pattern, slavery, had ended violently. Another method of social
hierarchy was being constructed, and it was erected also through violence. Coincident with the increasing participation of African Americans on the stage in the aftermath of the Civil War was an explosion
in the number of lynchings, with African Americans as target, occurring
in often quite public fashion across the country. Some lynching celebrations drew as many as ten thousand attendees, and photographs from
the time document the throngs that came to see the spectacle of death.[5]
The lines of limited possibility for African Americans were being drawn
in blood. In the cross-country barnstorming campaign, the African
American performer was traveling through troubled terrain. Carlyle
Brown is one of the few playwrights to call attention to the danger of
lynching that early African American blackface performers faced in their
efforts to establish a public presence and push past the strictures of
stereotype.

Tommy Parker is set in a private Pullman car that serves as conveyance
and shelter for a troupe of black minstrel performers. Archie, Doc,
Henry, Percy, Soloman, and Tambo are not the only ones traveling in
the car. There is also Baker, their manager, who hires and fires, brokers
engagements, handles the books, sells tickets, and, when necessary,
serves as liaison with local officials and potentates. This administrative
paradigm, the Anglo in charge of African American talent and earning
the lion's share of the money, became entrenched in America in the
postbellum era. It also emblematized the status of the African American
community, which was not fully in command of itself, although it had
a bit more legal latitude than under the lash of slavery. African American
performers could not represent themselves in the fullness of their being
but were required, by custom and audience demand, to construct a mask
that suited expectation. Henry and Archie—the youngest and most recently hired member of the troupe—discuss the creation of an appropriate look for the newcomer, who is eager to make good in entertainment, just as Henry was all those years ago when he was shining shoes,
doing another version of blacking up, outside the opera house in Philadelphia. Now Archie will have to put a shine on his public mask, con-
forming to the desires that have been imposed on him by the past.

> HENRY: We gonna make you black.
> ARCHIE: Make me black? I am black.
> HENRY: You ain't black enough.[6]

Being born black was not sufficient. Blackness was what the Anglos said it was, what they wanted to see on the outside.

Representations of African Americans on the legitimate stage were, at that time, performed by Anglos in blackface. A few years before the date when the events in *Tommy Parker* transpire, Percy, probably the most talented and versatile of the six Parker minstrels, was an extra with a company, one of hundreds presenting *Uncle Tom's Cabin*, the most popular and longest running play of the nineteenth century, when one of the regular Anglo actors got sick, and Percy went onstage in the character of Uncle Tom, whose depiction as long-suffering slave is "continuous with the minstrel tradition," which enacts a dichotomy of inside from outside.[7] For Doc, another Parker minstrel, Percy's performance was a revelation, bringing to bear layers of meaning that he had never before considered. "The only hurt he ever felt was for other people," Doc remembered. "To him, his bond was with the Lord, and whether he was slave or free that was a constant. I just never looked at it that way before."[8] Being able to represent themselves in their humanity, however they defined it, was what a number of black performers were fighting to achieve. They wanted to occupy their own skin and personhood.

The events in *Tommy Parker* transpire thirty years after the Civil War, and the colored performer, as he was then called, was much in demand, most often for plantation extravaganzas, some of which employed hundreds of actors in menial parts. One such show, *South before the War*, traveled throughout the country in the 1890s in its own parlor car that bore the name of the company.[9] Tom Fletcher, a black minstrel performer with more than fifty years of experience and who had started his career in Kentucky in 1888, recalled, "Around about 1890, colored shows had developed such drawing power that managers and producers were scrambling for colored talent."[10] There was work for black performers but not for everyone. Businesses and crops had failed. The country was in the grip of economic straits; nostalgia was rampant. In *Tommy Parker* the bad times are symbolized by the intense cold that has the nation in its icy grip. Returning in the mind to better times constituted an escape. Minstrelsy, which was popular for such a long time, recalled earlier days, when cotton was blooming on the plantation. During the antebellum years, its most popular period, blackface minstrelsy generated "commanding narratives with closely watched conventions."[11] Minstrelsy codified how working-class Anglo Americans defined themselves, as differentiated from and superior to the enslaved and freed populations of African Americans. Jim Crow, the iconic impersonation on the min-

strel stage, became synonymous with African American difference, a distinction that was enforced through violence. Minstrelsy expressed and policed the performative borders that separated black from Anglo. It enacted what was permitted under Anglo authority.

By 1895, when the black minstrels in *Tommy Parker* arrive in town, *Jim Crow*, the animalized name signifying less than fully human status, was the popular term, derived from minstrelsy, for segregation, which decreed that the races had to inhabit separate spaces. Churches, cemeteries, courthouses, schools, theatres, parks, restaurants, hotels, water fountains, bathrooms, waiting rooms, roads, and sidewalks were "Jim-Crowed," and public transportation, buses and trains, had their Jim Crow sections. It is not only for convenience but out of necessity that the Parker minstrels are traveling in their own Pullman car. They cannot stay in any of the hotels in the towns and cities through which they pass. They must eat and sleep in the safety of the railroad car. It contains and borders their world. It is their private as well as their public sphere. Symbolically, minstrelsy, continued in the synecdoche of Jim Crow, refused the null or eviscerated body (denied political franchise) full and equal access to the public arena, which was considered the province of whitened immigrant and Anglo bodies. In the years when minstrelsy was king, black bodies, displaced by Anglos and immigrants who were largely Irish and German and Jewish, were designated as territory to be occupied, as well as marginalized.

In its premise that Anglo male bodies were the motive power behind all black bodies, minstrelsy set the standard for how the nonvoting null body, male and female, was to act and be perceived under the governance of an asymmetric social syntax. That body was never to receive the same respect, never to assert its face with pride, but always to cede right of way, step into the gutter, and adhere to the decorum of subservience. This disparity in treatment can be read in the way the six minstrels in the Parker Company are identified, without family affiliation and only by time-worn sobriquet or first name, as opposed to the manager, who is known respectfully by the last name of Baker, presumably prefaced as often as possible by *Mister*. Minstrelsy established a behavioral code, based on the assumption of racial inferiority that relegated black performers to the role of placaters, which African American performers were constrained to follow, evidenced by the requirement that they blacken their faces and remain happy and tranquil in their subservience. The African American performers submitted, for their survival and sustenance, to the laws of minstrelsy, but, under cover of the blackface mask, they sometimes devised ways to subvert its conventions, which mandated symbolic death or nullity for those who were descended from slaves. From the inside the most adept of them managed to transform the minstrel mask from abjectness into agency.

The Parker Company, which includes several stage veterans, principally Percy, the protagonist who is also a songwriter and actor, as well as Archie, the neophyte of the group, is very much a moneymaking venture, bringing in enough profit to afford a modern vehicle that provides the troupe not only transportation and some protection but also a modicum of class. The car's sleekness serves as advertising, letting the townspeople know that some well-traveled curiosities have come to call. The Parker minstrels, who have journeyed a long way from Philadelphia, through Ohio, Tennessee, Kentucky, and Kansas, have stopped for the night in Hannibal, Missouri, where they intend to entertain an audience in the local hall in a few hours. A former slaveholding community and Mark Twain's hometown, Hannibal is a minor stop on the performance circuit, not large enough to warrant a separate theatre or opera house. It is situated on the banks of the Mississippi, a river that pushes right through the heart of the country and represents borders and the rush of time—although time has not moved quickly in Hannibal.

Many of the residents still remember slavery and the measure of standing in the community as well as the buffer from the most distasteful labor it afforded even to the whites who were not wealthy. The kind of slavery in force in Hannibal when Twain, who took intense delight in minstrelsy, was growing up there, and up until the end of the war, was not the plantation variety. Rather, small business owners, men in the professions, and shopkeepers were able to lease slaves, many of them children, who would do the hard work of the household. Parenthetically, it was this frequent exposure to the child slave that more than likely inspired one of the enduring masterpieces of American literature, Twain's *Tom Sawyer*. Twain's appreciation for minstrelsy, which he considered a true and accurate portrait of the slave, was mixed with disdain for those who departed from the stereotype of disadvantage.[12] He wrote his mother in Hannibal, where he had first seen a minstrel show in the 1840s, complaining that free blacks in the eastern cities were doing better than some folks back home.[13] Being in possession of slaves made a decided improvement in the daily life of people in Hannibal, and they were hard pressed to easily renounce or distance themselves from prior comforts.

Minstrelsy, which Twain linked to the menial status of the bootblack, symbolized those times of privilege.[14] When slavery was legal, the enslaved or freed body was banished, except in rare instances, from the arena of public representation, which blackface minstrelsy signified.[15] After Emancipation blacks were no longer chattel to be purchased or rented but had gained some degree of autonomy, although the extent of that independence was constantly being adjusted and abridged.[16] In the 1890s, at the beginning of the reign of Jim Crow, there were few options open. Working as a servant on the trains, otherwise known as a Pullman porter, or sharecropping, farming someone else's property and making barely enough to feed the family, or traveling in style through the South as a minstrel performer were the few means of livelihood available. Those who had the talent tended to choose the latter, even if it meant increased exposure to the restrictive mores of the Anglo community. The excitement and constant change of location, as well as the chance to hone their expressive talent and rewrite the options of the future, appealed to quite a few, and they selected this means of livelihood, which could sometimes prove injurious to their health. The itinerant existence of the black performer, more lucrative than sharecropping, could be precarious. Despite the dangers, the black minstrels traveled on circuits that included cities and towns like Hannibal, where the demand was strong for the type of old-time fare they offered. Only the biggest stars performed in the metropolitan centers, but even stars had to serve an apprenticeship. And touring was where they earned their experience.

Tom Fletcher, who spent his life touring, remembered how the railway car would often jolt on the tracks, speeding the black performers quickly to safety outside the city limits, away from the appeased audiences who no longer were that happy to have unknown dark faces in their town: "After the show . . . all the colored people connected with the show would get together and parade down to the car. If there were no trains leaving that night we would hire an engine and get right out of town without delay."[17] As newcomers and strangers in town, minstrel performers represented alien outsiders. Their presence was potentially combustible, unpredictable: "Whereas once black people were greatly limited in the scope of their movements, centered around a plantation or small town, blacks were now abroad in the land. The runaway slave or the rebellious maroon of antebellum times had become the 'strange nigger'—the black vagrant of no fixed address."[18] These black minstrels around town without a visible leash, and beyond the reach of the plantation lash, could easily misbehave, it was thought, or otherwise refuse to follow the customs that maintained orderly relations between the races. They might refuse to step to the curb and surrender the sidewalk. They might forget to doff their hats. They might flaunt their city ways and their store-bought clothes. They might flash the diamonds sparkling in their teeth, which many of them wore as insurance against hard times, against the possibility of being abandoned by a manager unable or unwilling to make payroll. They might be disease carriers. It was not unheard of for black minstrel performers to be chased out of town or even worse.

Lynching, which publicly staged the hierarchical relations between the races, hit its peak in the 1890s.[19] Even though we do not know and probably never will know all the victims taken in the lynching craze, we do have some numbers, which provide an index to the degree of devastation. We also know that the 1890s, when *Tommy Parker* is set, represented the most virulent phase of the lynching epidemic in America:

There were 106 blacks lynched in ten southern states in 1892, more than any year before or since; 103 would be lynched by the end of the following year. The situation was so desperate, *felt* so desperate, that in 1893 Bishop Henry McNeal Turner of Georgia issued a call for a national black convention to discuss "the reign of mobs, lynchers, and fire-fiends, and midnight and mid-day assassins" terrorizing blacks across the South. "[I]t is known to all present," he thundered in his opening remarks, "that not a week, and at times scarcely a day, has passed in the last three or four years but what some colored man has been hung, shot or burned by mobs of lynchers."[20]

The climate of lynching factors into the play, and the Parker minstrels have cause to feel uneasy. They are at risk. The scent of death is pervasive. Baker, the only one with connections, money, authority, and the protection of a white skin, has left the men with no plans for a quick exit from danger. Most likely he is lying on his back in a hotel room enjoying the charms of a good-time girl. His virtual absence from the play also works to underline the confederacy, the bond between the black performers. Momentarily, they are left to their own devices. They possess a space of autonomy. Percy, the most seasoned performer in the troupe, has also disappeared. As Doc, Henry, Archie, Tambo, and Soloman wait for Baker and Percy to return, they while away some of their time by listening to Tambo read the obituaries in the *Clipper* of several black performers, one of whom was shot inadvertently in the foot. The demise of this unfortunate man was brought about by being in an unlucky place at an inopportune time. The same could be said of the Parker minstrels stranded on the rails in Hannibal without an engine or a brakeman. A mob is milling around outside the car, and its presence casts a pall over the future.

Literally and figuratively the minstrels are surrounded by the reach of death. The company is named after a dead black minstrel that no one, except Archie, has ever seen. Baker chose Tommy Parker's name as a mask that could be manipulated to meet his needs, similar to the way Anglo minstrels treated the features and look of blackness as expedient disguises for their own purposes. But Parker is more than a ghost to Archie, who continues to be inspired by his skill. Archie, the untested member of the troupe and the one who symbolizes the continuance of the tradition for a new generation, wins the impromptu cakewalk contest the minstrels devise as a way of stoking their talents before the evening's performance. He attributes his mastery to watching Parker in San Francisco: "I saw Parker do it. Lots a times. At Maguire's Opera House. Look like he was flyin'. . . . He was somethin' else."[21] Archie, a youngster with drive, has taken Parker as his role model, and he wants to fly, to defy gravity, to beat the odds and become a gleam in the eye of the future. For Baker the dead black legend is merely a convenience. In whatever town the troupe is playing, Baker prefaces each show with the news of Parker's death. He knows what his audience wants.

In its canonical format referenced in the presentation at the opera house in Philadelphia when Henry was a boy, minstrelsy symbolized the eradication of the enslaved from the public sphere. Audiences, the majority of whom are immigrant and Anglo, never seem to tire of hearing how Parker met his demise. The reported death of a black man, particularly one with a career in the public eye, is almost as good as the real thing. As a preface to each performance, Baker treats the audience to a new story of how Parker died. At one point he was the target of black-on-black crime; on another occasion he was brought low by a spiteful woman. He has also been the victim of various accidents involving an animal or his own personal negligence. Once, he went to the rescue of a white child who otherwise would have suffered a painful, fiery end and received death, rather than preferment, as his reward. Being able to hold in their minds the image of the suffering and death of a black man was consoling, a sign that the social order was in its fixed and upright position. It was the duty of the subservient other to protect white life and to be punished by death if that honor were refused. Tommy Parker was acceptable because his death, always recent, brought to mind "the faithful old darkey keeping a sleepless vigil over his 'chillun,' whom he loved and for whom he would consider death a small sacrifice."[22]

The ignominious death of a scapegoated black male served as a protective talisman. However bad their circumstances might be, they were confident they would never occupy the bottom social rung. That space was taken. There was someone lower they could taunt and kick, someone they could band together and kill without penalty as the ultimate expression of the privilege they shared. They empowered themselves by disempowering those they ostracized. The world was awry, off kilter, when blacks exhibited too much prosperity, a sight that made Mark Twain fidget after he left Hannibal. The minstrel paradigm legislated that Africans were impoverished emotionally, psychologically, intellectually, physically—in every way that mattered. The Anglicized performers painted their faces black and gave their Anglo audiences a demonstration of the bumbling inferiority of blacks, who represented perpetual lowliness. Losing the war and having to contemplate the political and social worth of former slaves staggered the South, and the North did not escape unscathed. The anxieties devolving from the uncertainties of the era were deflected onto the black body, easily targeted as the cause of the problems. At the end of the nineteenth century the old hierarchy was fighting for maintenance. The agrarian lifestyle, which had depended on slavery, was losing ground to the urban, horses were being replaced with the accelerated speed of automobiles and trains, the night was electrified, the human voice was traveling over long distances, and the medium of film, then in its infancy, was about to steal the spotlight from its theatrical parent. Seeing the face of the past fade into the distance can be unsettling, and it often reinforces a desire to stay entrenched in the known. Fear has a similar stultifying impact.

Doc, Henry, Archie, Tambo, and Soloman, the minstrels who are stuck, without a train scheduled to leave that night or an engine to which they can hitch their car, occupy themselves by talking about past exploits even though trouble is pungent in the air. Punctuating their reveries, Soloman, who has an appetite for reality, explodes at Henry, "What am I worryin' 'bout? . . . Henry, you got a memory short as the hair on your head. I suppose you wasn't over there cowerin' in the corner when we come rollin' in here today and them people was shootin' at this railroad car. I guess you blind and can't see these bullet holes in this here parlor car."[23] Their vehicle has been damaged in this town, and they are vulnerable. The local residents are ambivalent about these newcomers, these modern and dissembling black men that they see as upstarts. The townspeople can't be described as welcoming and hospitable. Neither can the February weather. For two weeks it has been bitterly cold, the coldest it has been in years. Ice is on the tracks, and the bullet holes perforating the private Pullman car won't allow the heat from the stove to stay inside.

The minstrels are having a hard time staying warm, and they huddle together, not just because of the cold. To bolster their spirits and let them know that escape is possible, Soloman recalls a time, five years before, when the coat of a Pullman porter saved a black minstrel named Jimmy Rogers from being lynched. Rogers was traveling with the legendary W. C. Handy, author of the *Memphis Blues* and the *St. Louis Blues*, when a couple of the minstrels were diagnosed with the pox. The people in that Texas town quarantined all the minstrels, held them captive in their railroad car without food or water. Rogers let himself out the trapdoor, which in some cases also held provisions and weapons, and put on the coat of a porter.[24] The crowd took one look at that coat and determined that this was a colored man committed to giving service. They trusted him and let him go. They were convinced he knew his duty and would cater to their desires before his own. He was able to get to the next town and let a touring minstrel group there know what was going on. They came and staged a parade, and in the hubbub and commotion the other black minstrels still in the car were able to slip out the back and escape, disguised as women.[25] Soloman says he still has that coat, and that's his protection. When Percy returns, frozen to the bone, he brings bad tidings. He is a hunted man. Once again it is Soloman who sums up the situation. "They was waitin' for one of us to get out a line, from the first. They wants to see a show alright. They wants to see some niggers dance. See 'em dance in the air, from a rope."[26]

In the 1890s the practice of lynching started its transition, via technological advances, into modern spectacle entertainment capable of attracting and indoctrinating thousands about the worthlessness and sacrificial status of the black body.[27] Countering that message, insisting on one's self-worth was a dangerous stance. Refusing to cower was sometimes all it took for a black body in the South, especially if it was stray, to become prey for the lynching noose. Such a body, particularly one already employed to entertain the public, could be immediately apprehended as grist for the mill of southern example. These dark-skinned traveling minstrels in the Parker Company are new in town, known and protected by no one except Baker, the manager, himself a stranger who could be lynched if he refused to comply with local command. As the modern era dawned, the technologies of travel and communication were transforming the everyday, and the public sphere was in the process of being renegotiated as well. An opening or rupture occurred in the aftermath of the Civil War, which spelled the death of the plantation economy. This rupture made it possible for new constituencies to emerge, but their ascendance was opposed. Those formerly in social ascendance came together, sometimes in violent aggregation, around the notion that the new world would replicate the boundaries and divisions of the old. Segregation stepped into the shoes of slavery, and lynching, the enforcement arm of apartheid, was loose in the land, ever on the lookout for the next black body to string up, literally, as cautionary example.

The defiant ones who resisted the status quo of black on the lowest rung of the social ladder were targets for reprisal. The black minstrel performer, who simultaneously represented the adventurous and the abject, had to walk a difficult tightrope between pleasing the audience with his virtual or his actual death. The play dramatizes this reality. In the crackling cold the Parker minstrels are waiting on the tracks, surrounded by southern residents hungry for warmth, hungry for excitement. Percy tempted the unimaginable. He defied local custom. He went out in public too well-dressed for a black man. He was seen on the main streets taking a pleasure stroll and eating ice cream with a willing young colored lady from town. He was advertising his sexuality and his prosperity, and some of the residents in Hannibal, enough to constitute a crowd, felt aggrieved. The black stranger had transgressed the limits. He was not playing the inept minstrel who could barely string his words together with sense, the impecunious wastrel with holes in his pockets, the minstrel they could poke fun at and treat as the target of derision. They accosted him, pelted him with snowballs, knocking off his hat, and he fled into a theatre. When the mob pursued him there, he pulled out his gun, a symbol of his manhood and his citizenship, his right to protect himself from harm. He was cornered, and he fired back in retaliation. He didn't shoot anyone, but he dared resist capture and immediate death by mob. He fled into the cold and found a hiding place near the docks.

After several hours passed, he knew it was time to return to the parlor car. Fears, no doubt, raced through his mind. Would he have to entertain the crowd stirring outside with his skill as a performer or with his death? He is by no means the first entertainer of color to be confronted with a similar predicament. At one time or another W. C. Handy, James Weldon Johnson, Ethel Waters, and Williams and Walker, as well as many others whose names are not so well known, faced profound racial challenges in the late nineteenth century and early twentieth. In Duluth, Minnesota, in the summer of 1920, three black men—Elias Clayton, Elmer Jackson, and Isaac McGhie—roustabouts for the John Robinson Circus, were lynched by a mob five thousand strong after being accused of raping a white woman, a charge later determined to be unfounded.[28] In the thirteenth chapter of his autobiography, Handy recounts a catalog of "outrages and grim hateful crimes" that begins with the head of a black man being tossed like a ball into a group of black men standing on Beale Street, matrix of the blues, as a reminder of what could happen to them if they didn't mind their manners.[29] It's no wonder that some minstrel performers got in the habit of keeping a gun. On another occasion, in Tennessee, Handy had to hide in the trap space of a railway car to avoid detection by the local sheriff after he had done the unthinkable of raising his hand against a white man. There is a secret space in the Parker car too, but it is an escape hatch, not a hiding place or sanctuary, as it functioned for Handy.

It is possible that playwright Carlyle Brown, who has a definite interest in black performance history, read Handy's autobiography. The story of Louis Wright parallels closely what Percy tells his fellow performers when he returns. Wright, a talented musician, possessed a strong sense of pride that would not allow him to eat crow; that wording reveals a connotation of Jim Crow as someone expected to subsist on a diet of insult. Louis was on his way to a theatre in Missouri, in the company of a lady friend, when he cursed the men who flung snowballs at him:

> That night a mob came back-stage at the theatre. They had come to lynch Louis. In his alarm the sharp-tempered boy drew a gun and fired into the crowd. The mob scattered promptly, but they did not turn from the purpose. They reassembled in the railroad yards, near the special car of the minstrel company. This time their number was augmented by officers. When the minstrels arrived, the whole company was arrested and thrown into jail. Many of them were brutally flogged during the questioning that followed, but no squeal was forthcoming. In time, however, Louis Wright was recognized. The law gave him to the mob, and in almost less time than it takes to tell it they had done their work. He was lynched, his tongue cut out and his body shipped to his mother in Chicago in a pine box.[30]

In Brown's version Percy finds a way to slip past the mob. In the eyes of the citizens of the town his crime was that he bought ice cream and walked on the sidewalk with a girl of his own race from Hannibal. He was pursuing pleasure, which violated the minstrel code that yokes the black self to Anglo control and profit. Then he turned on and cursed the men who forced him and his lady companion to the curb and then threw snowballs at him, knocking off his hat. He managed to elude capture. "That mob was dead behind me," Percy tells the other minstrels, who understand very well that his actions have imperiled them all. "And every now and then I could feel some of they hands grab for me and slip off. . . . The theatre was just up the street. I barely managed to turn into the door, much less close it behind me and drop the latch. . . . But they broke it down and pretty soon they had me cornered in the aisle. I had no choice then. I had to pull out my little rascal and fire on 'em."[31] The space of the theatre offered him momentary protection and a place to take a stand. Then he went to the streets near the river, where he hid in a cold packing crate for hours, long enough for the mob to dissipate. Back in the provisional safety of the Pullman car, he must figure out how to remove himself from the dilemma he faces. The mob wanted, and still wants, his death. He has breached custom. He dared to parade his prosperity, dared to enjoy himself promiscuously in public, dared to defend himself, dared live the citizenship and privilege his color denied him, dared take the mask of public subservience off his face.

Through the character of Percy, Carlyle Brown turns inside out the question of ownership that lies at the root of both the lynching ritual and the traditional minstrel performance. Lynching, a rite of dismemberment, took hold of the black body as communal property belonging to and subject to partitioning by the federation of whiteness. The Anglo minstrel performer took over and claimed the look, sound, and movements of the black body, thus asserting his authority and ownership. A symbolic skinning, minstrelsy treats the black body as a collection of parts, which can be disintegrated, exaggerated, manipulated. Percy decides to participate, willingly rather than begrudgingly, in the minstrel ritual of pulling apart his integrity. He will submit to mock mutilation and manipulation onstage in order to survive. He will not run. He knows he wouldn't get far. To his advantage, he will use the minstrel expectations of the audience and reclaim ownership in himself. He will achieve this through blackface. By choosing to apply blackface to answer his purposes rather than the agenda of others, Percy asserts control over his behavior, from which he will extract pleasure and profit. He will no longer be the pawn of others. He will apply blackface as a shield against the probing eyes of the crowd. The look he will create on the outside will belie what exists on the inside. He will exploit the inside/outside dichotomy of minstrelsy to his profit rather than to his detriment. He will take the poison and turn it into the cure. Usually, in the performances of the minstrel troupe Percy takes the role of the interlocutor, the master of ceremonies who is not masked. He functions as the man nominally in charge. Tonight he will not assume that role. Instead, he will play the jester, the clown. By choice and for the sake of expediency, he will blacken his face and exaggerate his lips. To save his skin, Percy will resume the mask. Reminiscent of the Pullman porter coat that Jimmy Rogers wore in Texas to fool the mob, the mask of subservience can be protective. As it served the antebellum Anglo minstrels who put on the skin and guise of the other, the mask can magnify the wearer, especially if the one electing to employ the mask does so to camouflage intentions, separating the outside appearance from the inside reality. The mask can reduce vulnerability. Symbolically dying through putting on the mask of the outsider, Percy can stage the desire of the audience and still keep his life. Under cover of the blackface mask Percy goes out to meet the crowd, thus placating their desire for blood and titillating them with the stereotypical images of his virtual death, which minstrelsy represents.

The Parker minstrels have covered much distance, literally as well as figuratively. They have traveled miles and miles through unwelcoming territory, and they have negotiated difficult borders, especially the toll road between life and death. With Percy as catalyst, the one among them who takes the biggest risk, they go on with the show despite the odds and in the face of the lynching threat, pushing forward an agenda of African American continuance and survival in and through performance. In *Tommy Parker* Carlyle Brown reveals the complex and contradictory nature of minstrelsy. Yes, it was procrustean, requiring that, under penalty of extreme sanction, African American performers fit themselves to the standard measure set by Anglo artists and practitioners. In an art form that bears and promotes their image, African Americans were not the final arbiters. Their authority was secondary in a genre that represented them to the world. Minstrelsy functioned as the gateway, or rather the eye of the needle, through which African American artists proceeded to gain a modicum of economic, cultural, social, and political wiggle space for themselves—symbolized by the Pullman car—where they could set about crafting, in the interstices of possibility during a transitional time, a public identity in greater, but still constrained, consonance with their needs and circumstances.

Notes

1. Brown also authored *The African Company Presents Richard III*, which is focused on backstage tensions at the African Grove, the early-nineteenth-century black theatre founded by William Alexander Brown, playwright and theatre manager. The African Grove, which was open to interracial patronage, was so successful in the early 1820s that Brown was able to build a three-hundred-seat theatre in what is now Greenwich Village, where he offered productions that asserted the democratic right of African Americans to stage their own autonomy and participate in the same kind of theatrical offerings that the rest of the country enjoyed. Stephen Price, the manager of the Park, the leading theatre in New York of the day, more than likely paid the police to harass the African American actors at the Grove and close the theatre. Its productions

were reviewed in the press, and the company is credited with giving training to two major African American Shakespearean actors. One of them, James Hewlett, stayed in the United States and was frustrated in his efforts to establish an independent career. Ira Aldridge left America for England, where he appeared first in 1825. After that he became one of Europe's most popular Shakespearean performers. He died in Poland in 1867. What Carlyle Brown dramatizes in his play about the African Grove—that some authorities with pull were so outraged by the self-possession and achievement of the members of the company that they or their agents pursued them and pushed them outside the public sphere—is repeated, to some extent, in *Tommy Parker*, except that the threat to the company does not end in eradication. By the end of the nineteenth century the African American performer was able to acquire greater entrée into a more limited social and cultural terrain. Carlyle Brown has written other plays as well, including *The Negro of Peter the Great, The Pool Room, The Blue Nail,* and *Buffalo Hair.*

2. Quoted in Eric Lott, *Love and Theft: Blackface Minstrelsy and the American Working Class* (New York: Oxford University Press, 1993), 37.

3. See Krin Gabbard, *Black Magic: White Hollywood and African American Culture* (New Brunswick, NJ: Rutgers University Press, 2004), 43.

4. W. T. Lhamon Jr., *Raising Cain: Blackface Performance from Jim Crow to Hip Hop* (Cambridge, MA: Harvard University Press, 1998), 215.

5. See James Allen et al., *Without Sanctuary: Lynching Photography in America* (Santa Fe, NM: Twin Palms, 2000).

6. Harry J. Elam Jr. and Robert Alexander, eds., *Colored Contradictions: An Anthology of Contemporary African American Plays* (New York: Plume, 1996), 129.

7. Lott, *Love and Theft,* 33.

8. Elam and Alexander, *Colored Contradictions,* 103.

9. The papers from the *South before the War* company are located in the Irving S. Gilmore Music Library at Yale University.

10. Tom Fletcher, *The Tom Fletcher Story: 100 Years of the Negro in Show Business* (New York: Burdge, 1954), 53.

11. Lhamon, *Raising Cain,* 76.

12. There is some disagreement on this point. A number of scholars argue that Twain was a master of satire, which he used to pointed effect in critiquing contemporary attitudes toward blacks.

13. Bernard Bell, "Twain's 'Nigger' Jim: The Tragic Face behind the Minstrel Mask," *Mark Twain Journal* 23, no. 1 (1985): 11.

14. "Twain . . . observes that minstrels had 'buttons as big as a blacking box,' collapsing blackface masquerade, the means of its artifice, and an echo of one of its literal sources—Negro bootblacks—in a single self-conscious figure" (Lott, *Love and Theft,* 30–31).

15. Emancipation arrived earlier in the North than in the South. In Boston, for example, slavery was outlawed by the end of the eighteenth century. In New York all slaves were free by 1827. Even before then in New York, an emerg-

ing black middle class expressed a taste for the theatre. It was from this group that the African Grove, mentioned above, was born, only to have its institutional life ended in untimely fashion.

16. Grace Elizabeth Hale, *Making Whiteness: The Culture of Segregation in the South, 1890–1940* (New York: Vintage, 1998), 200.

17. Fletcher, *The Tom Fletcher Story*, 58.

18. Philip Dray, *At the Hands of Persons Unknown: The Lynching of Black America* (New York: Random House, 2002), 75.

19. Hale, *Making Whiteness*, 201.

20. Adam Gussow, *Seems like Murder Here: Southern Violence and the Blues Tradition* (Chicago: University of Chicago Press, 2002), 65.

21. Elam and Alexander, *Colored Contradictions*, 122.

22. Dray, *At the Hands of Persons Unknown*, 75.

23. Elam and Alexander, *Colored Contradictions*, 105.

24. Handy recalls, in his autobiography, how the custom Pullman car in which his company of minstrels was traveling throughout the South used the crawl space beneath the car to keep supplies, food, and water. See W. C. Handy, *Father of the Blues: An Autobiography* (New York: Macmillan, 1941), 45.

25. Doing this put them in unlikely company. Jefferson Davis put on the clothes of a female and attempted to escape after the Confederacy fell. His disguise was not successful, and he was apprehended.

26. Elam and Alexander, *Colored Contradictions*, 125.

27. Hale, *Making Whiteness*, 203.

28. Allen et al., *Without Sanctuary*, 175.

29. Handy, *Father of the Blues*, 179.

30. Ibid., 43.

31. Elam and Alexander, *Colored Contradictions*, 126.

The Role of William James Davis in the Rise of Chicago Touring Theatre

Jane Barnette

T HE IMPORTANCE OF THE railroads to touring theatre seems obvious enough. Without train routes theatre troupes could not travel. Beyond merely enabling tours, though, trains affected the very ways theatre was created and received. Scholars in film and gender studies have already begun writing this history—of how railroads (as a concept and as a business) affected early filmmaking and fin de siècle expectations of gender behavior. Lynne Kirby's *Parallel Tracks* (1997), for example, argues that "the railroad should be seen as a *protocinematic* phenomenon," one that we must recognize as "a social, perceptual, and ideological paradigm" with considerable influence on how early film spectators saw the world around them.[1] Although she never mentions live performance, Kirby's methodology, which draws on Walter Benjamin, Roland Barthes, and Michel Foucault, frames her project in ways similar to those underlying my own research, insofar as I work to understand the cultural impact of railroads on theatre production.[2]

Scholars of American culture and history help to flesh out these questions further. A full review of the literature exceeds the purview of this essay, but I do want to draw attention to the work that historian Amy Richter has done to further the inquiry of how railroads affected the performance of everyday life for American women at the beginning of the twentieth century. Her award-winning dissertation, "Tracking Public Culture: Women, the Railroad, and the End of the Victorian Public," challenges the separate-sphere ideology so pervasive in feminist histories of this period by "tracking" the "complex and contradictory ways Victorian Americans accommodated the anonymity, social diversity, and technological uncertainty of modern life."[3] To do so, Richter relies on both archival and secondary sources, including contemporary periodicals, correspondence, and railroad paraphernalia.[4]

In the field of theatre and performance studies, scholars have yet to apply the methodology of cultural studies to railroad touring per se. Thus far, railroads have been studied as a character or metaphorical image in performance but not as a factor in theatre economics or production. In surveys of theatre, historians consistently mention the importance of the rails to this transition, but it remains a peripheral point of interest for them.[5] Not so for me. My research seeks to answer the question "How did railroads affect Chicago-area theatre?" In what follows I focus on the unlikely success of the Chicago Church Choir Company's tour of *HMS Pinafore* in 1879 as a case study to explore this question further. The manager of this tour, William James Davis, became a pivotal figure in what Alfred Bernheim labels "the industrial revolution of the theatre."[6] As a Chicago-based affiliate of the Theatrical Trust (or Syndicate), Davis eventually left the road to manage two key Syndicate venues, the Illinois and the Iroquois theatres. Moreover, after the initial success of his *Pinafore* tour Davis married Jessie Bartlett (the actress who played "Little Buttercup" in the 1879 tour), who would herself become famous for singing "Oh Promise Me" in *Robin Hood* during an 1891 nationwide tour with the Bostonians.[7] Will Davis's records, most of which were donated to the Chicago Historical Society (CHS), reveal a telling glimpse into how touring theatre became a crucial part of making American mainstream theatre the profit-driven enterprise it remains today.

At the crossroads of Chicago-area railroad and theatre history, then, was Will J. Davis, who described his association with both of these businesses accordingly:

In 1873 . . . [Davis] entered the freight service of the Lake Shore Railway from which he was induced to go into the box office of the Adelphi Theatre. . . . In the Winter of 1876 he took the original Georgia Minstrels to California for Haverly & Maguire. . . . Jan. 1, 1877 he returned to the Lake Shore Railway at the solicitation of some strong personal railway friends and became Assistant General Passenger Agent of that road. In 1878 he was selected by a combination of trans-continental railways and Atlantic and Pacific steamship companies to go to Australia to endeavor to secure European travel by the American route. . . . Returning to Chicago in 1879, he was sought by Colonel J. H. Haverly who . . . wanted [him] to assume the active management of [the American tour of Her Majesty's Grand Opera Company] and as the inducement was good pecuniarily he returned to the amusement field never again to leave it.[8]

I quote this autobiographical excerpt at length to demonstrate the rhetorical equivalency of these career choices—"from which he was induced" —indicating not just the similarity between the professions but also the assumed understanding of such a link. In other words, Will Davis did not consider it odd to join theatrical management after working for the rails; indeed, he found it *more profitable* to do so. Moreover, while he refers to his role as manager of Her Majesty's Grand Opera Company, he omits mentioning another major event of 1879—his (Haverly-sponsored) tour of *HMS Pinafore*.

Why would Davis overlook such an unlikely success? After all, in 1879 *Pinafore* was all the rage. Without protection from international copyright law this Gilbert and Sullivan operetta spawned thousands of American interpretations, especially after R. M. Field brought *Pinafore* to popular attention in 1878 at the Boston Museum.[9] As a contemporary critic claimed, after Field's success, "'Pinafore' companies sprang up like mushrooms; actors who couldn't sing, singers who couldn't act, and novices who could neither sing nor act were hastily banded together and hustled out 'on the road,' scuffling and elbowing for precedence, and eager to obtain the first grab at the rural shekels."[10] In this context the challenge of mounting a successful *Pinafore* tour became all the more daunting. But Will Davis had advantages that few other novice theatre managers had: he had worked for the railways, so we can logically assume that he had insider's knowledge about how to negotiate contracts and plan the most profitable routes.

Although he may have neglected to mention the tour in his "Sketch of Life," Davis took care to memorialize this production of *Pinafore* inside a clothbound, hardcover blue book labeled in gold letters "Scrap Book." For today's reader, opening Davis's scrapbook in the Chicago Historical Society's reading room initiates an uncanny glimpse into the livelihood of this man. I notice where he hastily attached a clipping here but lovingly arranged another page there. In retrospect, however, I am struck by the homogeneity of its contents. Rather than preserving programs, correspondence, advertisements, and the like, he chose to designate this book solely for reviews and a few editorial columns. Near some of the clippings, Davis took care to note the name of the newspaper, but many remain unidentified, and few are dated. In fact, even those articles with dates are rarely in chronological (or any other obvious) order, making the journey through the scrapbook impressionistic and nonlinear.

Of all the snippets Davis kept, the editorials regarding the origins of his tour seem most out of place: they are, after all, the only dissenting perspectives included in his scrapbook. Described as a "mutiny" by both the *Chicago Tribune* and the *Louisville Courier-Journal*, the initial production of the choir's *Pinafore* was apparently managed by Finney and Curry, a Chicago-based theatre management team.[11] In June of 1879, according to these accounts, the show opened at Haverly's Chicago theatre to a mild midweek success, hitting its stride by the weekend. At the outset Finney and Curry engaged the choir at Haverly's for one week, with an option to renew after this interval. Unsure of the staying power and profitability of this nonprofessional choir, the managers were hesitant to renew the contract, and during their lapse Haverly's booked other shows. Since Haverly's was booked for most of July, Finney and Curry attempted to secure dates for *Pinafore* to play at a competing venue, McVicker's. But Will Davis was too quick for Finney and Curry, and he secured a contract with the Church Choir Company to play on the road under his management and Haverly's auspices. Technically speaking, the actors were under two contracts, each of which had equal "hold" on their performances and pay. They banded together under Davis's leadership, but this move was harshly criticized, and Finney and Curry threatened to sue Haverly, Davis, and the actors. As Thomas Finney wrote in a letter to the editor of the *Chicago Tribune*, "common social and business courtesy required that [the choir] should have at least advised us of their intentions, especially as they had led us to believe in every way that conversation could indicate that they were with us—a unit—as to our future plans."[12] Misunderstandings aside, the company members had violated their contract with their original managers. Surprisingly, however, there do not appear to have been legal ramifications for the choir's decisions.

Railroad barons were infamous for similarly sneaky maneuvers. In the early 1850s, for example, the Michigan Southern railway (to which Davis would later have ties) refused to allow the Illinois Central to cross its tracks. According to legend Michigan Southern positioned a guard at the requested intersection to protect the company's route, but Roswell Mason (then at the helm of the Illinois Central) arranged to have the guard kidnapped one night, and by morning a "railroad frog" allowed the Illinois Central to cross Michigan Southern's tracks whenever it pleased.[13]

Eventually, larger companies like the Illinois Central and the New York Central subsumed the smaller local upstarts like the once-rivals Michigan Southern and Michigan Central, both of which would become part of the New York Central line. The strength of the Michigan Southern route was its east-west straight shot between Chicago and New York, along Lake Erie, through Toledo, Ohio. In his autobiography Davis recollects how his father helped build part of this route before "the panic of 1857 broke the railroad and likewise his father who was then building the Air Line division from Elkhart to Toledo."[14] Years after the New York Central bought out the Lake Shore and Michigan Southern railway, it began to advertise the "Air Electric Line" Will's father had helped build. Even after it changed hands, then, the strength of this route remained the east-west road.

Haverly's Chicago Church Choir traveled along this road, although it also used the Chicago and Rock Island route and what appears to be the Illinois Central. Throughout Davis's scrapbook various reviews from different city newspapers list the upcoming (or recently traveled) tour for the show, such as this one, listed in the *Chicago Tribune*: "Louisville, Ky., Sept. 22–27; Nashville, Tenn., 29–30; Evansville, Ind., Oct. 1; Terre Haute, Ind., Oct. 2–4; Vincennes, Ind., 3; Springfield, O., 6; Columbus, O., 7–8; Indianapolis, 9–11; Fort Wayne, 13; Toledo, 14–15; Detroit, 16–18; Grand Rapids, Mich., 20–21; and Jackson, Mich., 22."[15]

Given the speed of travel in 1879, virtually every moment between stops would have been spent on the train, although the Haverly's sponsorship made it possible for the actors to travel by special (often Pullman sleeping) car. The route itself seems typical, in terms of the time spent at each venue and the types of cities chosen, except for a few telling variations—in particular, going from Vincennes, Indiana, to Springfield, Ohio. The choice to stop in Springfield seems odd (why not just go the distance to Columbus?) until railroad routes are considered. Springfield was a railroad hub and had been since the Old National Road was completed there in 1839.[16] In railroad maps of the period Springfield remains a key destination from which travelers could choose a variety of destinations.

Towns like these were ideal for smart businessmen who wanted to maximize profits. As show towns they might only warrant a "one-night stand," but as railroad centers they offered options: from Springfield, Davis could reassess his tour and decide whether to take the choir to St. Louis or Toronto. He decided on the latter, perhaps because from Jackson, Michigan, he was closer by then—perhaps Jackson was chosen because it was en route to Canada—either way, Davis plotted his tour so that he could rest not just in big show-towns but also in railroad hubs.

The contracts and booking systems of this period reinforced Davis's ability to identify and maximize profit. His "Little Buttercup" for *Pinafore*, Jessie Bartlett, signed a contract typical of the period, which included this closing clause: "This engagement to be binding *for a further period of three, six or twelve weeks on my option*. Miss Jessie F. Bartlett agrees that she will not appear in any other entertainment or with any

ILLINOIS THEATRE

Jackson Boulevard, near Michigan Avenue, Chicago

THE ILLINOIS is one of the few monumental theatres of America, there being no other occupancy. Because of the peculiar stone of which it is constructed, the theatre constitutes the distinct architectural attraction of the city.

Dedicated Oct. 15, 1900, by Miss Julia Marlowe, in "Barbara Fritchie," under direction of Charles Frohman, who also gave the suggestion of the theatre's name. Mr. Davis superintended the construction and arrangement of the house.

Amusement Co. of Illinois
Klaw & Erlanger, Wm. Harris, Harry J. Powers, Will J. Davis and Chas. Frohman, PROPRIETORS
WILL J. DAVIS - - Manager

The Amusement Company of Illinois. Undated ad in M. B. Leavitt's *Fifty Years of Theatrical Management* (New York: Broadway, 1912), n.p. Collection of the author.

other managers either before or during the term of this engagement without my permission."[17] This "on my option" clause demonstrates how Davis (and others in his position) assured financial protection—if the tour bombed, it could be canceled, roles could be reassigned, or the route could be changed, according to the manager's whim. Unfortunately, actors (who were not paid for rehearsals) were often stranded when shows were canceled, since their transportation was only covered during the run (that is to say, success) of a show.

By the beginning of the twentieth century the Theatrical Syndicate made this sort of manager/producer-oriented philosophy its policy, hiking share rates as high as possible to its benefit and canceling shows with little notice if they stopped turning a profit. By 1900 Will Davis officially joined forces with the Syndicate's Al Hayman and Chicago impresario Harry J. Powers, working as the house manager of the Illinois Theatre, under the auspices of the Amusement Company of Illinois.[18] On January 25, 1900, a letter requesting "open time" at Greene's Opera House arrived in Cedar Rapids, Iowa. It was from Will Davis, manager of the Columbia, the "leading theatre of Chicago," and the letterhead noted Davis's affiliation with Hayman. The stationery touted the Davis-Hayman empire on its reverse, claiming cooperation with theatres in Nashville, Louisville, Toronto, Minneapolis, and Indianapolis. Most of the cities on this letterhead backside were ones Davis had toured with the Chicago Church Choir's *Pinafore*.

In this way Davis's railroad connections came full circle: they had introduced him to Haverly and would help him book a successful tour, and now he returned the favor, establishing these same show towns as part of his powerfully connected chain. From his downtown Chicago offices Davis continued to distribute entertainment and build new theatres for the Syndicate monopoly, to great profit, for some years to come.[19]

Although causality is more diffuse than direct, and dedicated historians should try to resist our "legacy of seeking to drive out commanding narratives,"[20] the connection between Will Davis's past as a railway agent and his later work managing profitable tours and playhouses offers insight into how we understand the economic history of American theatre. In other words, Will Davis's archives support part of our traditional narrative of American theatre history: that late-nineteenth-century theatre practices established the patterns of touring commercial theatre still common today. Arguably, however, the railroad industry's influence went further than affecting touring or business practice. It seeped into how we see and understand actors and performance itself. Part of the reason *HMS Pinafore* sold tickets was that the lyrics were "catchy"— patrons left the theatre humming the tunes and remembering the words. For example, during the tour Jessie Bartlett reportedly profited from her growing celebrity status, becoming a spokesperson for the fabric manufacturer Corticelli.[21] Not only did she wear a costume spun by this brand of silk, but also she broke the monotony of the well-known musical by inserting an advertisement for the silk. This was easily accomplished, since Buttercup's aria lists the things she sells ("I've snuff, and tobaccy, and excellent jacky; I've scissors, and watches, and knives"), but it was innovative enough to gain public favor. Her commercial couplet "I've nice apple jelly / And silk corticelli—" reportedly induced the audience to a standing ovation, "and the effect was heightened by the charming 'Little Buttercup' offering each sailor of the gallant crew a selection of beautifully colored, dainty silks wherewith they might clew up their fore-garnets or perform other nautical evolutions."[22] The review never clarifies whether Bartlett sold these silk wares to the audience or only onstage, but she reportedly gained public favor "by the cheap rates at which she offered Corticelli Spool Silk for spot cash."[23] Similar to those who sing commercial jingles on television today, early-twentieth-century American actors were a vital part of the capitalist system. Further, the songs they sang were known well enough that phrase substitutions could be inside jokes for spectators. In turn, these actors gained celebrity power and could demand higher pay—Jessie Bartlett, who would marry Will Davis by the end of the tour, became the first Chicago-area actress to make one thousand dollars a week in vaudeville. What I mean to suggest is that the repercussions of this period can be felt even now—in ways that continue to affect how we do, see, and think about theatre—even if today we hardly notice the whistle of a train or the sound of a locomotive crossing the tracks. Even if railroads have faded largely from our cultural memory, the power of "selling it"— both literally and figuratively—certainly has not.

Notes

1. Lynne Kirby, *Parallel Tracks: The Railroad and Silent Cinema* (Durham, NC: Duke University Press, 1997), 2–3. Lynne Kirby is a filmmaker and producer who currently serves as the vice president of alternative programming for Court TV.

2. See Jane Barnette, "Locomotive Leisure: The Effects of Railroads on Chicago-Area Theatre, 1870–1920" (PhD diss., University of Texas at Austin, 2003).

3. Amy Richter, "Tracking Public Culture: Women, the Railroad, and the End of the Victorian Public" (PhD diss., New York University, 2000), 20. Richter, an assistant professor at Clark University, was awarded the Lerner-Scott Dissertation Award from the Organization of American History (OAH), a group committed to promoting "excellence in the scholarship, teaching, and presentation of American history" ("Mission Statement," OAH Web site, http:// www.oah.org/about/mission.html [accessed Nov. 9, 2004]).

4. The etymology of *paraphernalia* is itself gendered, for the term derives from the Latin shorthand for *paraphernalia bona*, or paraphernal goods. Legally, the term came to mean "those articles of personal property which the law allows a married woman to keep and, to a certain extent, deal with as her own" (*Oxford English Dictionary*, 2nd ed., s.v. "paraphernalia").

5. Barnard Hewitt's relatively short chronicle of theatre, *History of the Theatre from 1800 to the Present* (New York: Random House, 1970), implies the importance of the railroad: "After mid-[nineteenth]century, with the continued improvement in transportation and the progressive deterioration of resident companies outside the large cities, it became profitable to send an entire company on tour" (33). Oscar Brockett takes the railroad development into consideration in his explanation of U.S. westward expansion in the mid-nineteenth century and in his explanation of the shift to combination company touring practices. See Oscar G. Brockett, *History of the Theatre*, 7th ed. (Boston:

Allyn, 1995), 401, 405. In *Theater in America: 200 Years of Plays, Players, and Productions* (New York: Abrams, 1986) Mary C. Henderson acknowledges the importance of the rails: "It occurred to several of [the managers] that since the railroad had shortened distances between cities, a theater cooperative or 'circuit' would induce the New York producers to give them firm bookings and a better deal" (25). These excerpts are typical of survey texts: all recognize the importance of the transportation revolution to the business history of American theatre, but the authors rarely devote more than a sentence to discussing how the routes enabled major shifts in theatrical production to occur.

6. Alfred Bernheim, *The Business of the Theatre: An Economic History of the American Theatre, 1750–1932* (New York: Blom, 1932), 31.

7. The Bostonians were a traveling repertory troupe based on the D'Oyly Carte management system. Richard D'Oyly Carte, the business manager (and, after 1881, proprietor of the Savoy Theatre) for Gilbert and Sullivan, not only made more money than either artist he represented, but he also helped maintain control over their copyrights. For more on D'Oyly Carte and Gilbert and Sullivan see Alan Jefferson, *The Complete Gilbert and Sullivan Opera Guide* (New York: Facts on File, 1984).

8. William J. Davis, "Sketch of Life," 2 (an autobiographical manuscript written in third person), William James Davis Papers, 1879–1914, qF38DA D29, Chicago Historical Society (CHS).

9. Under Field's management the Boston Museum's acting company gained a solid reputation, but it "disbanded in 1894 and the theatre fell into the Theatrical Syndicate's hands until [the theatre] was razed in 1903" (Don B. Wilmeth, ed., *Cambridge Guide to American Theatre*, rev. ed. [Cambridge, UK: Cambridge University Press, 1996], 72).

10. Press clipping from the *Detroit Post*, Oct. 19, 1879, in "Scrapbook of William J. Davis for 'The Chicago Choir Company in *Her Majesty's Ship Pinafore*'" (52–53), qF38 RN C43 D6, CHS.

11. The theatrical management firm of Finney and Curry rarely mentions the first names of these partners, but elsewhere (in M. B. Leavitt's tome on theatrical management, for example) mention is made of Thomas J. Finney. I was unable to find Curry's first name. In all my records, when he is referred to without Finney, he is called "Mr. Curry."

12. Davis, "Scrapbook," 39.

13. This rogue crossing point was wildly dangerous; in 1853 a collision killed eighteen passengers, leading the public to demand regulations regarding right-of-way passage. See George H. Douglas, *Rail City: Chicago, USA* (San Diego, CA: Howell, 1981), 42–43.

14. Davis, "Sketch of Life," 1.

15. "At Home. The End of the Pinafore Season," *Chicago Tribune*, Sep. 21, 1879, in Davis, "Scrapbook," 34.

16. See City of Springfield Department of Information Technology, "History," http://www.ci.springfield.oh.us/profile/history.html (accessed Sep. 25, 2004).

17. William J. Davis collection, CHS (emphasis added).

18. The logistics of this coalition remain uncertain. Davis claims in his autobiography that he joined Hayman and Powers (4), but contemporary ads for the Illinois Theatre call the union the "Amusement Company," listing Powers, Klaw and Erlanger, Frohman, and William Harris but not Hayman.

19. Will Davis's influence did not wane until after his Iroquois Theatre burned in 1903, killing nearly six hundred people, mainly women and children. Davis escaped legal ramifications for his part in the fire, although his reputation (and his marriage to Jessie Bartlett) suffered greatly.

20. Rosemarie K. Bank, "Representing History: Performing the Columbian Exposition," *Theatre Journal* 54 (2002): 590.

21. I define *celebrity* along the same lines that Richard Schickel does, insofar as it entails "the principle [*sic*] source of motive power in putting across ideas of every kind—social, political, aesthetic, moral" (quoted in Neal Gabler, "Toward a New Definition of Celebrity," *The Norman Lear Centertainment,* http://www.learcenter.org/pdf/Gabler.pdf, 13 (accessed Sep. 25, 2004).

22. Davis, "Scrapbook," 30.

23. Ibid.

The National Black Theatre Festival

A One-Stop Tour

J. K. Curry

L AST AUGUST I WAS SITTING on a plane on a runway at LaGuardia waiting for a thunderstorm to pass so that we could take off for Greensboro, North Carolina. Several passengers, on their way to the National Black Theatre Festival (NBTF) in Winston-Salem, expressed their concern about possibly missing the celebrity-packed, opening-night gala. Four hours into our wait, when the plane was finally brought back to the gate, I knew at least one passenger was worried about missing more than the gala. William J. Vila (a.k.a. Triple-5), the stage manager for a play called *Monk*, had a performance scheduled the next day at 3 p.m., with load in to begin at 11 a.m. After a few more delays in the terminal, our flight was cancelled. Most of us were re-booked on flights late the next day. That schedule obviously wouldn't work for Vila. After extensive conversations with airline employees, he finally arranged to get to Greensboro using an indirect connection, starting with a very early morning flight, which he would stay over at the airport to catch. There was still the matter of retrieving our bags, which turned into another several-hour delay as airport workers apparently did not notice that our plane had not been unloaded. Many fellow passengers gave up on getting their bags back that day, but, of course, the stage manager carrying props and music CDs for the show in his luggage needed to track down his bags. In the end Vila did make it to Winston-Salem, about three hours before his first scheduled perform-ance, and was able to call the show. Load in and adjustment of light cues had already been started by actor Rome Neal, who had arrived earlier the previous day, and Trevor Anderson, technical director at Wake Forest University, where the performance occurred. Anderson observed that Vila was obviously an experienced stage manager, well acquainted with this production, and able to jump in at the last minute and run the show without a hitch and with the audience unaware of any potential problems.

I share this anecdote because the event challenged my notion that touring was only difficult in the "old days" of travel by wagon, steamboat, or train. It also made me give the National Black Theatre Festival more thought, realizing that the whirlwind of theatrical activity does not just magically appear every two years in the town where I live. Rather, it is a logistically complex enterprise that involves travel, not just for the majority of the productions being staged but also for a significant portion of the audience. In effect, it functions as a one-stop tour, bringing together enough theatre productions and other attractions to draw an eager audience and providing enough of an audience to make it worthwhile for productions, even some not originally designed to tour, to make the effort to travel to Winston-Salem. Normally a tour requires multiple stops to find audiences and make a profit. Despite operating as a single stop, the NBTF can be thought of as a tour because all the personnel and production elements have to be moved long distances and loaded into new venues on a tight schedule. Staging a play at the NBTF involves much of the logistical complexity encountered by productions that tour multiple cities, as opposed to productions staged only at a company's resident theatre. The NBTF also functions like a tour for its audiences in Winston-Salem, who catch the performances passing through town. Audiences, whether permanent residents of Winston-Salem or festival visitors, have a unique opportunity to see companies from out of town, but only for a limited engagement.

By bringing productions and audiences together, the National Black Theatre Festival raises the visibility of black theatre, not just in the Southeast but nationally. The festival develops and supports a sense of community and camaraderie, providing extensive opportunity for networking and development. Producers and theatre companies use the festival to find additional venues for a production or financial backing for a tour. So although the NBTF is only a one-stop tour, it often leads to more extensive touring for individual productions. Writers present new, previously unproduced, plays in the readers' theatre series with the hopes of getting their work staged, and actors use the exposure to find additional work. In addition, the National Black Theatre Festival provides a boost to the local economy and is supported by the City of Winston-Salem as a means to promote travel and tourism to the area and to enhance the reputation of the city.

The National Black Theatre Festival was founded in 1989 by Larry Leon Hamlin and is held every other year in early August. Hamlin, also the producer and artistic director of the North Carolina Black Repertory Company, first had the idea for developing the festival while researching black theatre in the South for an article he wanted to write. Discovering that most southern black theatres were in terrible financial shape, he extended his investigation to other parts of the country and learned that small black theatre companies across the country were struggling to survive.[1] The NBTF was conceived as a way to raise the visibility of black theatre and to bring theatre artists together to network and share expertise. The initial plan was for a one-time event. In an interview Hamlin said, "None of us knew what to expect because we'd never done it. So as the festival bloomed and flowered we were watching it like everyone else."[2] The first festival featured thirty-one performances of productions by seventeen theatre companies, including the Negro Ensemble Company, Crossroads Theatre, Cultural Odyssey of San Francisco, the Penumbra Theatre Company of St. Paul, the Philadelphia Freedom Theatre, the Just Us Theatre of Atlanta, and the Harlem Jazz Theatre.[3] Sponsoring such an ambitious festival just once seemed almost beyond the reach of the North Carolina Black Repertory Company. Hamlin said, "Because we were a small company we never had more than say $10,000 worth of debt. But after our first festival we were $165,000 in debt. Of course, we paid it off. That really expanded our ability to raise funds. We never would have thought that we could raise $165,000 to pay off debt but we did—or that we could raise half a million dollars."[4] In fact, the budget for the 2003 festival, which included more than one hundred performances by thirty companies, was about 1.5 million dollars.[5]

In addition to realizing he could raise the money, Hamlin discovered an unmet need. He said, "We were just feeding the hunger that was there. There was a profound need for this festival."[6] Some eight thousand to ten thousand people showed up for the first NBTF. That was many more than expected and, according to Hamlin, resulted in the local hotels running out of food and liquor. Hamlin himself was surprised by the turnout: "I thought that only people in the theatre would come—actors, directors, producers, an autonomous group—but no the general public said we're coming to this also."[7] Of course, Hamlin also admits he should have suspected the public would want to attend, as from the first the festival has made a point of featuring celebrity guests. Winston-Salem resident Maya Angelou served as chairperson for the first festival and helped to attract other celebrity guests, including Oprah Winfrey, Ruby Dee and Ossie Davis, Louis Gossett Jr., James Earl Jones, and Cicely Tyson. The event drew national attention with a feature article in the *New York Times* in which August Wilson is quoted as saying, "This is the kind of thing that I've sat around for the last 10 years saying should happen. That all the people involved in black theater in America should get together, simply to understand that we're not working in a vacuum, that there are other companies out there and that they're doing the same thing you're doing."[8]

The enthusiastic reception of the first festival demonstrated a demand for more such gatherings. The festival format made it easy for theatre professionals and other interested audiences to see several theatre pieces, potentially the best current work in black theatre, in one city within a span of a few days. The festival provided a fairly convenient format for companies to showcase their work to a wider audience, beyond their local communities. And by coming together the theatres were collectively able to achieve greater visibility on a national level. Another important need the festival has fulfilled is to provide a sense of community, especially for those working in or hoping to make a career in black theatre. From the beginning Hamlin billed the NBTF as a "celebration and reunion of spirit."[9] The point of the festival has always been more than just bringing plays and audiences together. In addition to the theatre productions, the NBTF has regularly offered workshops, colloquia, networking opportunities, and the chance to socialize with old friends and rub elbows with celebrities, informally and at big events like the opening gala. Bringing the critical mass of people to one spot allows participants to experience a sense of community.

Having a production accepted for presentation at the NBTF gives companies from around the country an opportunity to showcase their best work and raise the profile of their theatre. Almost all of the mainstage productions selected have been mounted at least once previous to the festival. (An exception would be new work developed by the North Carolina Black Repertory Theatre to premiere at the festival.) Hamlin or one of his associates usually travels to see the original production before an invitation to the festival is issued, although occasionally productions have been selected on the basis of a videotape submission. According to NBTF technical director Arthur Rees about 50 percent of the productions selected were not originally designed to tour and have to be redesigned to travel to the festival.[10] Once the effort is undertaken to bring a show to the festival, many producers hope to make arrangements to tour the productions in other cities. Some even look to find additional backers to mount more elaborate productions of the plays in new venues. Quoting Hamlin again: "Do those companies that come here use the festival as a spring board? Well, of course they do! And now most of the companies that come here are interested in touring anyway, so this is just a great place to come because you can network with other theatre companies that are interested in bringing shows in or presenters that would have an interest and, of course, a lot of deals are made at the festival."[11] Arthur Rees estimates that 95 percent of the productions at the NBTF are hoping to arrange for further touring.[12]

Hamlin cites an example of a production that picked up momentum for its tour after proving a hit at the festival: "In 2001 we had *The Jackie Wilson Story*, a company out of Chicago, no one knew about them. They came here and just blew up large, so large that in less than six months they were playing in New York."[13] This is not to say that *The Jackie Wilson Story* owes all its success to the NBTF. The musical, written and directed by Jackie Taylor, began its run at the Black Ensemble Theatre of Chicago in February 2000 and ran for more than two years. The appearance at the NBTF did seem to facilitate a tour, and the production appeared in a number of cities, including Memphis; Baltimore; Washington, DC.; Norfolk and Richmond, Virginia; Detroit; and Louisville, with a two-week stint at New York's Apollo Theatre, before the show's young star, Chester Gregory II, moved to Broadway as a replacement in the role of Seaweed in *Hairspray*.[14]

A somewhat different use of the festival to develop and promote a play is seen in the example of the play *Monk* by Laurence Holder, which was performed at the 2003 festival. This one-man show about jazz legend Thelonious Monk featured music by Bill Lee and starred Rome Neal (who was also awarded the Lloyd Richards Directing Award during the festival). The play was first presented in New York City at the Nuyorican Poet's Café in 2000. Positive reviews suggested the play could find a wider audience. Holder and Neal, serving as codirectors, revived the piece on a couple of occasions, including at the temporarily reopened Crossroads Theatre in New Jersey in 2002. By the time they brought the play to the NBTF, they had bigger plans. After each performance Neal invited audience members to consider investing in an Off-Broadway production of the play with a contribution of one thousand dollars for a share. (Note that this show was brought from New York City to North Carolina to raise money for future, larger NYC production.) Promotional postcards also directed patrons to a Web site, where they could review the proposal and budget.[15] Although the desired Off-Broadway production has not yet been realized, the project is still under consideration. Also, as a result of the festival, Rome Neal did a production of the play in Detroit during February 2004.[16]

Another way the NBTF encourages more productions is through its reading series. According to Hamlin, "the playwrights are really looking for someone to produce their shows. It starts out here as a reading and then it usually—most of the shows, if they are good, will find legs as a main stage production in one of the black theatres in the country. If it continues to do well there it will move around to other black theatres in the country."[17] So for many participants the festival can lead to additional opportunities to present their work in new places. As Hamlin sees it, "Everyone gets a chance to make some type of deal here or at least present it. The players are here."[18]

Despite being a tour of just one stop, the NBTF is nonetheless logistically complex. There are the usual problems of touring as all the production elements have to be transported, plans made in advance to adapt to new spatial configurations and dimensions, and load ins accomplished in four to twelve hours, depending on which slot a production is scheduled to fill. The festival staff makes arrangements with each production to move required scenery. For example, the festival usually sends three truckloads each year from New York and two or three from the Atlanta area, each truck holding the equivalent of two to three box sets.[19] Though there have been travel difficulties, such as the example I mentioned at the beginning of this chapter, technical director Arthur Rees says, "Amazingly enough we have never missed a performance."[20] On top of the travel challenges, of course, is the difficulty of opening fifteen or more shows simultaneously and replacing them two to three days later with another set of productions. The festival uses virtually every available theatre space in Winston-Salem, including those on the campuses of the North Carolina School of the Arts, Winston-Salem State University, and Wake Forest University, and has also started using hotel ballrooms as theatre performance spaces. As much as possible problems are solved by advance communication and negotiation about any unusual technical requirements. Rees also stresses the importance of hiring individuals he knows as problem solvers to work with him at the festival, since he cannot be at all venues simultaneously.[21]

Of course, many more people travel to the festival than just the performers and production staff of the main-stage theatre selections. Hamlin estimates that only about three hundred or so of the festival's attendees are directly involved in the productions.[22] Other attendees include prizewinners and celebrity honorees; workshop, seminar, and colloquia presenters and participants; college theatre companies presenting as part of the festival's fringe; and writers and performers participating in the play-reading series, storytelling festival, or late-night poetry jams. Many more people attend solely as audience members. Total attendance estimates for the 2003 festival ranged from twenty-five thousand to more than forty thousand.[23]

Winston-Salem is not a major tourist destination. Perhaps because of this, city and county officials and local corporate sponsors have taken an interest in the traveling audience the NBTF draws. With a conservative attendance estimate of nine thousand overnight guests staying in hotel rooms and another sixteen thousand day guests, Forsyth County's Tourism Development Authority put the direct spending impact of the 2003 festival at 11.4 million dollars.[24] The day guests are not all local residents. Many drive in from other parts of North Carolina and from Virginia and South Carolina; and even if they do not stay in hotels, most spend money on food, gas, and other available local resources during their visit. With an interest in encouraging visitors, the City of Winston-Salem was one of the major sponsors of the festival in 2003, providing a grant of one hundred thousand dollars. The city has traditionally also helped with in-kind support in the form of street closings, extra police staffing, and special signs.[25] For example, a major thoroughfare in Winston-Salem, University Parkway, temporarily bears signs labeling it "Black Theatre Festival Boulevard." Of other major sponsors in 2003, some were businesses aimed at African American consumers, for example *Black Enterprise Magazine* and the *Electronic Urban Report*. Many other sponsors were businesses with a significant corporate presence in Winston-Salem, including R. J. Reynolds Tobacco, Wachovia, Bank of America, GMAC Insurance, and Sara Lee Branded Apparel.

In addition to the direct economic impact, the sponsors seem to be interested in the indirect effect of the festival in enhancing the image of Winston-Salem as a desirable place to visit and live. The NBTF ties in to local efforts to promote Winston-Salem as a "city of the arts." The mayor of Winston-Salem, Allen Joines, a prominent supporter of the festival, has identified several reasons for the city and local businesses to support the NBTF:

There are many intangible benefits to the festival. As we move our economy to a more "knowledge based" one, the type of companies we are recruiting are looking for communities that offer a high quality of life and embrace cultural diversity. Certainly the NBTF contributes to both of those issues. In addition, it offers an opportunity for our own citizens to come together in a neutral atmosphere to explore broader cultural experiences. I believe this type of festival helps our racial issues as well. Finally, it gives Winston-Salem national publicity for the time of the festival. For instance last year we had a reporter from the *New York Times* here who did a very positive article on the festival and on the city.[26]

Joines went on to say, "It is also important to our City Center revitalization effort. Last year I was chairman of the fund raising for the festival and was pleased at the strong support of the business community."[27] Hamlin notes that support for the festival from the local population also seems to have grown since 1989: "We're still in Winston-Salem, we're still in the South, all of those things, even though somehow Winston-Salem has made a promise—unspoken, unwritten—that during that week of the festival, everyone—this city—is on its best behavior. It's all about Southern hospitality—black, white, it doesn't matter. Of course, that makes it very enjoyable for the festival attendees."[28]

As Winston-Salem has come to see the value of hosting the festival, other cities have attempted to persuade the festival to make their city the only stop on the tour. Hamlin has been invited to several places where city and corporate sponsors were willing to put up money to attract the festival with its tourist revenue and its perceived ability to enhance the reputation of the host city. One city that approached Hamlin about relocating was San Jose. According to Hamlin,

> They don't really have very many black people, maybe 2 per cent something like that. They were interested in changing their image. They said we are known as the Silicon Valley, technical, but we want people to know that we have culture as well. That's what you can do for us. We don't want any change, just do exactly what you are doing. I said, but you don't have any black people. They said, don't worry about that.[29]

Of course, in considering requests from prospective host cities, Hamlin has several factors to weigh. For one, he estimates that he needs fifteen hundred dedicated volunteers to run the festival. He has that reliable support in Winston-Salem, a city of about 185,000, which is nearly 40 percent black. Hamlin also recognizes that the support of the artistic community is vital, as he needs to use various organizations' and schools' theatres and get all the groups to buy into the idea of supporting the festival. While Hamlin says he has received some good offers, so far none have been able to compete with the proven support in Winston-Salem. Another type of offer has been to bring the festival to a second city during the "off" years. This idea has not been pursued seriously by Hamlin, who along with technical director Arthur Rees, is already at work on the next festival about the time the previous festival ends.

So for now the NBTF is a tour that travels only to Winston-Salem. Local sponsors are happy to see not just the show but also the tourist audience come to town. And although the official "tour" is the shortest imaginable, many of the participants will use the event to keep their individual productions on the road and to find new audiences in different parts of the country.

Notes

1. Mervyn Rothstein, "Festival Sets Goal for Black Theater: New Togetherness," *New York Times*, Aug. 16, 1989, C17.

2. Larry Leon Hamlin, interview by the author, March 2, 2004, transcript, 12.

3. Rothstein, "Festival Sets Goal for Black Theater."

4. Hamlin interview, 11.

5. Richard Carver, "Theater Festival Brings $11.4 Million in Tourism Spending," *Winston-Salem Journal*, Oct. 22, 2003; and Jeanette Toomer, "Black Arts Festivals Celebrate," *Back Stage*, July 11, 2003.

6. Hamlin interview, 13. Hamlin contrasted the need for the NBTF with that for the Arts Ignite Festival held in Winston-Salem in 2002. The Arts Ignite Festival was much better funded in its first year, but it drew only a local audience. Hamlin suggested that this might be because it was attempting to fill a need already met by the Spoleto Festival in Charleston, SC.

7. Hamlin interview, 12.

8. Rothstein, "Festival Sets Goal for Black Theater."

9. Hamlin interview, 8. The festival is called "the mother of all reunions" by Rhodessa Jones in "The Mother of All Reunions," *American Theatre* 18, no. 9 (November 2001): 83–85.

10. Arthur Rees, email message to author, March 21, 2004.

11. Hamlin interview, 2.

12. Rees, email, March 21, 2004.

13. Hamlin interview, 2.

14. More information about the tour is available at www.blackensembletheater.org and www.kccall.com/News/2003/0103/Entertainment/009.html (both accessed Nov. 9, 2004).

15. Proposal and quotations from reviews are available at www.monktheplay.com (accessed Nov. 9, 2004).

16. Rome Neal, email message to author, March 22, 2004. *Monk* also had another run at the Nuyorican Poet's Café in July 2004.

17. Hamlin interview, 3.

18. Ibid., 2. For an additional example of producers using the festival to find investors see Perry Tannenbaum, "Black Empowerment Rules at NBTF," *Back Stage*, Aug. 15, 2003.

19. Arthur Rees, telephone interview with author, March 23, 2004.

20. Rees, email, March 21, 2004.

21. Rees, telephone interview, March 23, 2004.

22. Hamlin interview, 10.

23. Forsyth County Tourism Development Authority, "Estimated Spending Associated with the 2003 National Black Theatre Festival," puts the attendance at twenty-five thousand (report available from Forsyth County Tourism Development Authority, Forsyth County Government Center, 201 North Chestnut Street, Winston-Salem, NC 27101). Bruce Weber, "Black Theater: Beyond Definition," *New York Times*, Aug. 8, 2003, E1, estimated forty thousand attendees. Kelly Kramp, "Festival Draws Regional Crowd to Winston-Salem, N.C.," *High Point Enterprise*, Aug. 11, 2003, ventured a guess of fifty thousand.

24. Forsyth County Tourism Development Authority, "Estimated Spending Associated with the 2003 National Black Theatre Festival."

25. Allen Joines, mayor of Winston-Salem, email message to author, March 23, 2004.

26. Ibid.

27. Ibid.

28. Hamlin interview, 16.

29. Hamlin interview, 15.

The Black American's

Chitlin/Gospel/Urban Show

Tyler Perry and the Madea Plays

kb saine

A S A NEW (and white) drama teacher in the predominantly black Richmond City Public School system, I found myself faced with the challenge of creating a new curriculum for the 2002–3 school year. I mentioned my interest in beginning with the Greek plays to my advanced students and suggested *Lysistrata* and *Medea* as options; as soon as I said the word *Medea*, a palpable excitement filled the room. My students erupted: "I love Madea!" "That is my favorite play!" "I have it; can I bring it in? Can we watch it?"

I was instantly confused. How was it possible that my students, who had never read all of a full-length play, know, love, and own their own copies of *Medea*? I began asking: When did they learn this? In whose class? They stared at me in disbelief. They had not learned *Medea* in a class. "Everybody knows Madea!" they responded. One student pulled a VHS cassette out of his book bag and handed it to me. The cover read *Madea's Family Reunion* and prominently displayed a photograph of an older black woman, apparently dressed for church, but holding a gun in one hand and a cigarette in the other. My students immediately criticized my confusion: "How can you be a drama teacher and not know Madea?" "I thought you said you were a professional director!"

I thought I *had* known Medea, but clearly, this rendition was not aligned with the Greek text. I borrowed the video from my student, went home, and sat down to watch. I struggled to make the connection with the Greek story I expected and found myself at an absolute loss. This new Madea *was* driven crazy by her family, but the context was entirely dissimilar. The name alone (but not the spelling) is the common ground. This Madea, whose name is derived from the southern phrase "mother dear," or "ma dearest," is an entirely different entity.

The video was that of a taped stage musical—part gospel, part comedy, and reminiscent of a college-level production. The performance's redeeming quality lay in the character of Madea herself, the matron Mable Simmons, played by Tyler Perry in a fat suit and a very fun—and relatively convincing—drag costume. The film itself begged several questions: Is this strictly a popular cultural movement? Is Perry a black American folk artist? Does this performance provide an opportunity to discuss gender roles and identity with the black community, or does it serve largely as a morality play? How does Perry fit into the history of black theatre in America?

Advertisements for the Perry Corporation at the end of the video led me to search for some of these answers at the Tyler Perry Web site, which divulges a plethora of information, including a relatively lengthy and credible biography.

Thirty-four-year-old Tyler Perry, a New Orleans native, found success when his failing production of *I Know I've Been Changed* opened at the House of Blues in Atlanta and sold out eight times in a row. It then transferred to the Fox Theatre for a two-night run, where it sold out the nine thousand seats available. The play's first southern tour brought Perry to perform to a sold-out crowd in Dallas, Texas. In the crowd that evening was the Bishop T. D. Jakes, who immediately approached Perry about collaborating on a stage play based on Jakes's *New York Times* best-selling novel, *Woman, Thou Art Loosed!* The result was another successful touring play.

Focusing again on original work, Perry wrote, directed, and starred in his next production, *I Can Do Bad All By Myself.* Here lay his audiences' introduction to Madea. According to the Brokaw Company, "With the six-foot-five Perry donning a dress, wig, enormous bosom, cat glasses, and a handbag full of handguns, the brutally honest Madea became a sensation with the show's 2000 premiere."[1]

His company has since grown to tour seven gospel plays through American Theatre's Urban Circuit. With *Woman, Thou Art Loosed!* performing at the Apollo Theater and *I Can Do Bad All By Myself* at the Beacon, Perry has been the only black playwright to have two shows running simultaneously in New York. *I Can Do Bad All By Myself* earned Perry a nomination for the Helen Hayes Award for Outstanding Lead Actor for his Madea, the first nomination of its kind for urban theatre. His Madea character reappeared in *Diary of a Mad Black Woman* and met with such great success that *Madea's Family Reunion* and *Madea's Class Reunion* were written as showcases for the black "Mother Dear."

The Perry Company has since grossed more than fifty million dollars in box-office sales, and it claims that Perry's productions have played an integral role in encouraging critics' and historians' abandonment of the term "chitlin circuit" for the more politically correct "urban circuit."

The Brokaw Company's press release claims Tyler Perry's Madea "is as recognizable in the African-American community as Redd Foxx's Fred Sanford, Flip Wilson's Geraldine or any from Eddie Murphy." It is my personal experience that Perry's name and the Madea character are, in fact, even more recognizable, especially with black teens, who experience the plays first on video, commit them all to memory, and then flock—with their families—to the theatre when the chance arises to see the artist perform live. The Brokaw Company believes that "because of Perry, many African-Americans, from senior citizens to blue-collar workers to the hip-hop generation, have gone to the theater for the first time in their lives."[2]

Part of Perry's unprecedented success results from his ability to market his plays to the black American masses. Many of his greatest fans have never even seen a live production; his videos and DVDs have brought his plays into the living rooms of those who adore him. Joel Brokaw, Perry's publicist, reminds us, "Because of the culture of exclusion . . . African Americans did not feel invited to go to a mainstream theater and see a play" before Perry opened the doors to them.[3] These doors also lie at Perry's Web site, www.tylerperry.com, where his fans have instant access to tour dates, a message board where they can write directly to Perry, and opportunities to buy merchandise, including the coveted videos and DVDs. Brokaw notes that there are more than "280 thousand active members on [Perry's] Web site." Perry has sold hundreds of thousands of VHS and DVD copies of the four Madea plays; the official versions are available only through the Perry corporation, but the taped plays prove to be hot-ticket items: bootleg copies have become accessible on street corners, in flea markets and swap meets, and in barber shops across the United States. As a means of comparing Madea with other pop-culture icons, bootlegged copies of the Madea plays outsold even the infamous R. Kelly sex scandal tape in 2002.[4]

The Perry Web site's message boards prove the vast effect Perry's plays have had on the average black American's life. Here his fans clamor for more. Amid requests for tours to play in individual hometowns, for advice for amateur playwrights and actors, for appeals to Perry to meet talented family members of his fans, and even solicitations for marriage, testimonies reveal that Perry is making a difference in how black Americans view the theatre, in both recorded and live forms.

Cami McClain, from San Diego, California, asks Perry for a performance closer to home because although "I have seen them all . . . it means that I have to travel hundreds of miles to do so, not that you, the plays or Madea isn't worth it." Shelia G., of St. Petersburg, Florida, writes to Perry: "My family and I (23 of us) are attending your performance Feb. 18, 2004. . . . We enjoy watching your videos over and over again, especially my grandchildren." Here not only the broad reaches of Perry's influence but also the cross-generational audience he has created are expressed. A young child named Vene explains, "Me, Bianca, and Dewane which is my friends love your movies we even try to act them out especially my dad. My mom love it too."[5] Perry himself comments on the overwhelming familial connection blacks have found in his work: "I'm seeing Black families at my plays. I don't know of any other place than church where Black families are coming together."[6] Of the audience appeal, Brokaw notes, "This is about the broad base . . . about the masses."[7] American theatre has not yet experienced any other contemporary artist reaching this kind of mass appeal and mass popularity with the African American public.

Perry has "virtually reinvented theater for an often overlooked segment of the African-American population, many of whom are now regular playgoers for the first time in their lives."[8] His company reaches approximately twenty thousand to thirty thousand people each week with his live productions. His company claims that the mere mention of the name "Tyler Perry" in a playbill advertisement practically guarantees a sellout in several major markets. There is truth in this claim: "in January 2002, *Madea's Family Reunion* . . . sold out its twelve day performance schedules across the country a full month before its arrival in designated cities."[9]

My students were right: how, as a theatre professional, and as a historian, was it possible that I had never even heard of this man and his plays? How could such a successful movement in black theatre have gone unnoticed?

Historically, our black theatre has not successfully followed W. E. B. Du Bois's major principles of black theatre: that it be by, for, about, and near the black people. Where other black artists and companies have fallen short, Perry has—intentionally or not—succeeded. Perry, as a black man, provides a reflection of life to which many of his fans can personally relate. Perry has roots in a small, "shotgun" house in New Orleans. His background, professionally, is not rooted in theatre; in fact, his first writing resulted from his watching an episode of *Oprah*, where discussion addressed the cathartic effects of purging emotional scars through writing. A victim of child abuse early in life, Perry began his career as a means of coping with his own demons. Perry has always written what he knows; he writes from the perspective of the common black man. His goal is to reflect the reality that surrounds him, despite critics' responses that the stories are trite and mundane. In Margena Christian's *Jet* interview Perry states, "Some things aren't real that people are talking about. They think it's not legitimate theater, it's not reality. What reality is is what people are going through day to day."[10] This seems to be what the black masses crave: the ability to see themselves and their own real lives reflected on the legitimate stage.

Perry writes, also, *for* the average black man. Like his predecessors Willis Richardson and Randolph Edmonds, Perry sustains a "desire to treat the entire range of social, moral, and political problems that face black people, both as a group and as individuals." In some senses Perry also evokes some of the same ideals Langston Hughes had for writing plays for the black populace. Hughes "insisted that both the concerns of his works and the forms he used to express them be those of the ordinary black people he hoped would constitute his audience."[11] Perry uses Madea to that effect. The performance of *Madea's Class Reunion* finds Madea sitting at a table with all of the females, preaching about issues of domestic violence, relationships, drugs, sex, about choosing the wrong path, and about not learning from history and past mistakes. The lessons here are all endemic to black culture.

Each of the Madea plays remains *about* the black people. None of Perry's plays rely on history; they merely represent the black American world through his eyes. I suspect there is little difference between the conversations held in audience members' cars on the way to the theatre, and the onstage conversation inside. Onstage Madea gossips about Michael Jackson, pokes fun at Whitney Houston, and mocks the breadth of the behind and the 'bad weave' on the head of a nearby character. She bemoans the future of young black men in America and chastises the behavior of the grown black men. The significant difference in these conversations is in the witty, biting approach Madea is allowed.

The root of Madea's motivation for humor is also the root of these gospel plays' plots. Forgiveness is always the lesson. Madea explains to the females in *Madea's Class Reunion*, "Everybody got to learn the lesson. If not, they gonna stay right where they is."[12] Perry's gospel plays evoke a sense of Willis Richardson's early folk plays, where ordinary black folk are presented with dilemmas that require a moral choice, while dictating the "right moral choice" for each situation. The teachings of the church always prevail. Even if Perry's characters are flat and formulaic, they create a unique form of modern morality-plays. Perry says, "I'm not trying to impress anyone with my writing as much as I am trying to get people to think about their situation."[13]

Du Bois dictates that black theatre exists *near* the people. This is where many of our black theatre artists have fallen short but where Perry excels. He takes his plays to his people rather than forcing them to travel to unfamiliar areas; each of his plays departs his Georgia home base to tour much of the country in predominately black communities. When Perry first began touring, he and his company focused their efforts on showcasing these plays for the black people, in spaces accessible and connected to black audiences. *I Can Do Bad All By Myself*, Madea's debut play, appeared in Dallas, Texas, not at the city's major roadhouse but at the Naomi Bruton Theatre at the Black Academy of Arts and Letters. As his success has grown and he has needed larger venues, the Perry Corporation still makes wise choices, playing the Warner Theater in Washington, DC, the Murphy Fine Arts Center in Baltimore, and the Fox Theatre in Atlanta. The result is an increased loyalty from his audiences and greater success; he has established an audience of the faithful, and they have certainly proved a faithful audience. In only the first five months of 2004 his tour of *Madea's Class Reunion* included sold-out dates in Texas, Michigan, Indiana, Missouri, North Carolina, South Carolina, Florida, Tennessee, Kentucky, California, Louisiana, Maryland, Virginia, Washington, and New Mexico. Perry no longer needs to travel into the backyards of his fans; they will now travel to their cities' civic centers, convention centers, and coliseums to see him. And still, when his audiences cannot attend a live performance, the videos are readily accessible to satiate them.

Perry's goals echo a call given by his predecessors Willis Richardson and Amiri Baraka. For these men, too, the "aim was to make [their] work available to as many blacks as possible."[14] This widespread presence affords the major factors for the claims that Perry is responsible for changing the face of black theatre in America. His *is* the black face most Americans now see in our most popular black American plays.

My inspiration for this study was not spurred solely by my own ignorance about such a successful theatrical movement and the cultural phenomenon it had become but also by a statement I found in Perry's bio: that his plays have caused American theatre artists to "raise the level of thinking with regards to Black theater productions, [and that] critics and audiences alike would eventually abandon the insulting title of 'Chitlin Circuit,' when referring to Black theater, bestowing upon it instead the respectable title of 'Urban Theater.'"[15]

It is unclear where the rationalization for this argument originates, but Perry's efforts to maintain the integrity in his own contributions to black theatre are consistent. He realizes that "some critics have labeled urban plays in general unsophisticated, stereotypical and poorly written." He agrees with these critics to some extent. "Some of these plays give all of us a bad reputation,"[16] he says. He explained to Tom Sime, of the *Dallas Morning News*: "Before I got my chance to do this, I would go out and see these shows, and I would just be so aggravated, because I thought there was so much more that could be done. . . . I wanted to raise the standard."[17]

His major attempts at changing these standards have been in the scripts themselves, where, despite the one-dimensional characters, he has increased the complexity of the stories' themes and established heightened production values. Joel Hirschhorn's *Variety* review of *Madea's Class Reunion* calls special attention to the quality of "Peter Wolf's two-level hotel set, with its faux marble pink bar and registration desk."[18] Perry's plays all boast enormous, lavishly decorated, two-story sets, live music, and special lighting effects—qualities in the urban theatre that are unique to his productions alone.

Perry realizes the difficulties in attempting to produce a successful, legitimate play for an audience whose major theatrical outlets in recent years have been the action-filled narratives of Michael Mathews and Shelly Garrett's slapstick comedies. Perry has found himself lumped into this category by both black and white critics. Some, like Zondra Hughes, claim that Perry's career has marked "a new chapter in the urban circuit theatre as a whole—a genre that has been dogged by criticism from some Blacks in the traditional theater." Others "say Tyler Perry has set the Black race back some 500 years with these types of 'chitlin' circuit' shows."[19]

In his press release Perry explains: "A lot of Urban Theater is unsophisticated, stereotypical, and poorly written. Those shows drive me crazy because people work hard and pay their money and should get better. I've kept some of the overacting and what the audience expects but I think I've raised the bar."[20] What the audience expects from a gospel/urban musical, it seems, is more aligned with church services and stand-up comedians and improvisational sets, and the more frenetic call-and-response scenarios that often evolve from such performances than from a "traditional" straight play. Perry's gospel plays find obvious roots in the "chitlin circuit" history. Brett Collins explains the history of these gospel plays and the issues they raise:

Gospel plays came to prominence in the '90s, when Shelly Garrett, David E. Talbert and a few other enterprising writers decided to mount inexpensive productions that would serve an under-served demographic far removed from the Great White Way—black, church-going folks. What distinguishes "gospel" plays from regular musicals is the presence of "saved" characters who spout scripture and sing God-centered songs. They usually contain at least a couple of buffoonish, stereotypical characters, which led to the genre being widely derided as "chitlin' circuit theater."[21]

Tom Dent argues that there is an inherent, endemic need for this method, that "this is the Black style: emotion, broad humor, and individual improvisation against group harmony."[22]

Despite Perry's claims and attempts to change these conventions, he delivers this style unabashedly to his audiences, and the result is his plays' reinforcement of the gospel/"chitlin" stereotypes. Each of his plays features the "saved" characters, who use their prayer and witnessing to teach the moral lessons of each play. Inevitably, each moment of witness, and each epiphany, progresses as an actor or actress stands as far downstage as he or she can safely manage, singing and yelling through God-centered songs. Critic Kevin Johnson appraised *Madea's Class Reunion* as "a gospel musical at its core, which means a too-much-is-never-enough style of singing is used." He asked, "Why sing with any hint of grace when screaming and shaking go over so well?"[23]

In addition to the clichéd character of Madea Perry relies on the character of Mr. Brown to play the buffoonish, stereotypically ignorant, older black man. His costume, although disgraceful, is delightful: mismatched, ill-fitting plaid and striped shirts are coupled with high-waisted, flood-length pants that reveal white socks and ratty, old shoes. Brown seems at times to play the end man to Madea's interlocutor, as exemplified in *Madea's Class Reunion*, when she stands center stage and he takes stage left with a Pringles can in hand. When Madea asks him why he cannot put down the can, he adopts an exaggerated ignorance and dialect to explain that his wife's remains are inside and that he could not afford a better container. When his physical buffoonery gets out of hand, the can explodes and her ashes fly around the stage, Madea jokes about his marrying a "white woman." Theatrics like these, combined with gratuitous use of slang and improper grammar onstage and in print make it rather difficult to believe Perry is committed to breaking such stereotypes.(One ad gives the Perry Web site for ordering the Madea videos, and a phone number, too, "if you ain't got no computer.")[24]

Perry upholds Dent's prescription for black theatre with Madea's obvious improvisational escapades against the play's more formal script. These improvisational moments get so extreme that even Perry himself has trouble keeping to the script. At one point in a performance of *Class Reunion*, he realized, after a ten-minute tirade, that he was completely lost in his own text. Madea finally called out, "Help me here. You all see I forgot my lines!" and asked the other cast members onstage, "What my line is?" She then told her audience, "I'm gonna start all over—you all bear with me. If I can't remember it, I'ma gonna rewrite it, 'cause I wrote it all myself anyways!"[25]

In a separate improvisational tirade about the rap artist 50 Cent, she declared, "When you got talent, you don't need no gimmick." The irony is that Madea herself is all gimmick. Perhaps here, though, Perry provides his audience with some prescience about his efforts to deny the chitlin stereotypes his plays have endured, for *Madea's Class Reunion* is the last play Perry has written for the Madea character. But even without Madea Perry is finding success. His latest plays, *Why Did I Get Married?* and *Meet the Browns* are already selling out large theatre engagements, with only Perry's script and direction on the bill—not his performance. This departure from Madea has not been enough to ensure Perry legitimate status: "Even with his accomplishments, many don't acknowledge the Black traveling stage plays as real theater."[26] The credibility of Perry's urban plays as legitimate theatre continues to be questioned.

Perry is grateful for the Helen Hayes nomination: "What that did was give the rest of this 'legitimate' theatre an opportunity to say, 'Maybe before we criticize this, let's take a look at it.'"[27] August Wilson's endorsement does not hurt Perry's legitimate reputation, either. Wilson told Perry, "Do what you do. Don't worry about these people, do what you do because I don't think it's bad at all."[28] With each baby step toward legitimate acceptance Perry finds himself struggling against black and white theatre stereotypes. Tom Dent reiterates that the well-made play is not endemic to black culture. The well-made play seems, however, to still be the standard for judging white and black plays. Perry asks defiantly, "What makes your art any better than ours or what I do? Is it because 'the establishment' has told you this is the way [it's] supposed to be or how we do it? What makes that better than what's real to us as Black people?"[29]

We are left to debate not the authenticity of Perry's work but its place in the current, as well as historical, canon. Our own academic predispositions require us to label theatre and its performances. But with every label comes an inherent expectation, a typecasting established by the concurrent creation and definition of the label itself. Perry is most fascinating because he simultaneously defines and defies the "chitlin," "gospel," and "urban" identities. His preference, and that of his company, is obviously "urban theatre." Perry told the *Philadelphia Tribune*, "Since I've been on the scene, and I like to take credit for this, *American Theatre* magazine has abandoned the term 'chitlin' circuit' theatre, and started calling this theatre, 'Urban Theatre,' which is a wonderful thing, and I'd like to think that I had something to do with that."[30] Whether or not Perry has been the largest factor in this semantic change remains unclear, but Brokaw realizes, "When you achieve a certain level of success, the labels start to fall away, [and] you become a cultural phenomenon. . . . The categories and descriptors people use to explain you are not as necessary."[31] As historians, it seems that for now we will have to agree only that Perry is a Black Theatre Artist and watch as he works to break free from classification. The first task of scholars is to recognize and document this touring phenomenon as it continues to reach an American demographic largely unaffected by the more traditional foci of theatre history studies.

Notes

1. Tyler Perry, press release, Brokaw Company, Sep. 2003. The Brokaw Company is a personal management and booking agency in Los Angeles, CA.
2. Ibid.
3. Joel Brokaw, interview by the author, Jan. 14, 2004.
4. Brett Collins, "Tyler Perry's 'Madea' Revitalizes Genre," *Toledo City Paper Curtain Call*, Sep. 16, 2002.
5. Tyler Perry "Message Board," March 2004, http://www.tylerperry.com/message_center/forums/public (accessed March 15, 2004).
6. Quoted in Margena A. Christian, "Meet the Man behind the Urban Character Madea," *Jet*, Dec. 1, 2003, 64.
7. Brokaw interview.
8. Ytasha L. Womack. "Blackstage Passes," *Essence*, June 2000, 66.
9. Tyler Perry, "Perry Bio," Oct. 2003, http://www.tylerperry.com/411/biography/biography4.php (accessed Jan. 3, 2005).
10. Christian, "Meet the Man," 64.
11. Leslie Catherine Sanders, *The Development of Black Theater in America* (Baton Rouge: Louisiana State University Press, 1988), 20, 62.
12. Tyler Perry, performance of *Madea's Class Reunion*, Hampton Coliseum, Hampton, Virginia, Nov. 23, 2003.
13. Tom Sime, "Granny Get Your Gun," *Dallas Morning News*, April 2, 1999.
14. See James Haskins and Ted Shine, eds., *Black Theater in America* (New York: Free Press, 1996), 147.
15. Tyler Perry, press release, Brokaw Company, Sep. 2003. The terms *chitlin, gospel,* and *urban* are used interchangeably by the media in regard to the plays of these genres, but despite their own continued use of the other terms, the media continues to reprint the Perry Corporation's claim (as fact) that Perry's work is responsible for the move toward "urban theatre" as the appropriate label.

16. Womack, "Blackstage Passes," 66.

17. Sime, "Granny Get Your Gun."

18. Joel Hirschhorn, review of *Madea's Class Reunion*, Kodak Theater, New York, *Daily Variety*, Sep. 5, 2003.

19. Zondra Hughes, "How Tyler Perry Rose from Homelessness to a $5 Million Mansion," *Ebony*, Jan. 2004, 92.

20. Perry, press release.

21. Collins, "Tyler Perry's 'Madea' Revitalizes Genre."

22. Tom Dent, "Black Theater in the South: Report and Reflections," in *The Theatre of Black Americans*, ed. Errol Hill (New York: Applause, 1987), 266.

23. Kevin C. Johnson, review of *Madea's Class Reunion*, by Tyler Perry, Fox Theatre, Atlanta, *Post-Dispatch*, Oct. 30, 2003.

24. "Tyler Perry's *Madea's Class Reunion*: Theatrical Stage Production," http://www.Jade7.com, program, special edition, 2002, 29.

25. Tyler Perry, performance of *Madea's Class Reunion*, Hampton Coliseum, Hampton, Virginia, Nov. 23, 2003.

26. Christian, "Meet the Man," 62.

27. Ibid.

28. Quoted in Hughes, "How Tyler Perry Rose," 92.

29. Christian, "Meet the Man," 64.

30. Jade Designs, "Once He Lived in His Car; Now He's a Hit," *Philadelphia Tribune*, Jan. 9, 2001, 2B.

31. Brokaw interview.

The Farmville Opera House,

1885–1911

Bruce Speas

THE CHALLENGE OF ARCHIVAL RESEARCH is daunting but often rewarding. It is hoped that the following might provide some insight into the process. My discovery of the Farmville Opera House happened by accident. My search for a gift for a friend led me to a casual perusal of *History of Farmville Virginia, 1798–1948*, a book published by the town's local newspaper, the *Farmville Herald*. The text, examining more than a hundred years of publishing by the local paper, contained a copy of an advertisement that had originally appeared in the *Farmville Herald*'s sesquicentennial edition, published in October 1948. This advertisement was written to celebrate the two local movie houses, the State Theatre and the Lee Theatre, built in the 1920s and middle 1930s; but it also mentioned that prior to these two privately owned movie theatres, another theatre, "the Opera House," was constructed and owned by the town of Farmville: "In 1885 the Opera House was built. Road shows, traveling opera and stock companies were attracted to Farmville furnishing recreation to the townspeople. It was the center of social life when the 'opera' companies came to town periodically during the year. Community plays, public rallies, and political meetings were held there also."[1]

It was obvious that the Farmville Opera House had played a unique and important role in the lives and cultural cohesiveness of the community. The advertisement also mentioned that by 1921 the old Opera House had become outdated. The town of Farmville bought it and converted it into a municipal building for the town in 1927. Was that municipal building still standing, and if so, did the possibility of archival evidence still exist? Since the *Farmville Herald* mentioned the Opera

House, checking the microfilm of the newspaper's 1921 issues revealed a front page story in the February 4, 1927, issue announcing the conversion of the old Opera House into what was to become the Farmville Municipal Building. The fact that the municipal building still existed at the time of my research indicated the possibility of uncovering a nineteenth-century theatre in Farmville. My resulting excitement quickly vanished with an initial trip to the Farmville Municipal Building, however, where I discovered that the 1927 remodeling had destroyed all interior traces of the original second-story theatre and the businesses that had occupied the first floor. Only the external framework of the original Opera House remained. Of course, this initial walk-through of the building came without my having any in-depth knowledge of the old theatre space. Still, I thought that the task of trying to piece together evidence to gain an understanding of the physical theatre space that once existed and of the types of entertainment that played its stages was worth undertaking. Such understanding would not only shed more light on the role this theatre played in the history of the town but would also provide additional insight into similar activities that occurred in other small towns throughout the state of Virginia, the South, and the nation around the beginning of the twentieth century.

Uncovering information about such a public place proved difficult. Initial conversations with town officials elicited quizzical looks, and the fact that Farmville had ever had an opera house came as a surprise to many. I decided to begin my investigation into the Opera House by examining microfilm records of the town's newspapers. Longwood University, located in Farmville, keeps in its library microfilm copies of the town's newspapers beginning in the 1870s. Small-town weeklies such as that in Farmville contain a wealth of information on local activities. The planning, construction, and opening of such an undertaking as the Opera House would certainly be written about in great depth. Names, dates, descriptions would surely be included in the paper and would provide information and clues. In pursuing this avenue, however, I encountered a tremendous stumbling block. Microfilm records of the local weekly paper stop in 1873 and do not pick up again until 1893, under the banner of the *Farmville Herald*. A quick check of several local books written on the history of Farmville and the county of Prince Edward, Virginia, also reflected this gap in recorded history, a gap even more mysterious given that during those twenty years the town was served by a weekly newspaper called the *Farmville Journal*. Extensive library research and online investigation revealed that only four copies of that weekly paper exist, none of which are close to the year 1885. The hundreds of other issues have vanished. The *Farmville Herald* would prove invaluable in its weekly reporting of the activities of the Opera House from 1893. Many hours of microfilm research lay ahead, but I would need to explore other avenues as well.

One of the best ways to discover local information in a small town is to ask local citizens. This strategy led me to the Farmville Historical Society. The local historian knew of the existence of an opera house in Farmville, but its history had never been investigated. After several hours of researching the society's collection, I came across one major piece of information: a promotional brochure for the county of Prince Edward that had been published in 1888. This brochure yielded textual information and a line drawing of the Opera House as it stood in 1888. The drawing was extremely accurate in its detail and proved invaluable in comparing the original redbrick structure to the current one. A modern photograph was taken of the current municipal building from the same angle as that of the line drawing to make comparisons. Alterations in the brickwork of the 1888 second-story windows on the side of the Opera House were evident in the current building, giving an idea of the scale of the height of the auditorium's original windows. The 1888 front facade showed three entrances to the building: a large central doorway flanked by two smaller ones. In today's building the two flanking entrances are large windows, with the original center entrance still serving as the main entryway. I took a copy of the line drawing and the modern photo to a local architect, who provided insight into similarities and scale before and after the remodeling. He discovered that although the building had changed little, there was a slight difference in the roof structure. The remodeling had slightly lowered and lessened the slope of the original roof.

The text of the promotional brochure also gave insight into the value and reason for the Opera House's construction. My research into local census information had already revealed a period of growth during the late nineteenth century in the area. Population records showed that in 1885 the town of Farmville and the county of Prince Edward experienced modest growth, both in business and in immigration. The total population of the county in 1880 was 14,668 residents, and the population of the town of Farmville was around three thousand.[2] Building the Opera House was part of a campaign to bring new growth to Farmville. The county of Prince Edward mentioned this in the brochure: "Heretofore we have been denied the privilege of public and popular entertainments, but now our capacious and commodious Opera House has been completed, and we offer inducement, which we trust will bring to us the learned lecturer, the accomplished actor, the sweet singer, and give room enough for the vast audiences which are expected to gather within its walls from time to time."[3] For such a small town to have built an opera house would seem rather industrious, but this practice appeared to be common in small towns at the time, particularly those towns situated as stops along major railroads. The name *Opera House* was the title of choice for many of these theatres, whether they were large auditoriums or small, second-floor operations such as the one in Farmville.[4]

In doing general research on late-nineteenth-century opera houses and the booking companies that played them, I discovered *Julius Cahn's Official Theatrical Guide*, a yearly publication of theatres available for bookings. This guide lists and describes many theatres, academies of music, and opera houses from Maine to California. I discovered an advertisement for the Farmville Opera House in an 1896 edition of the guide, which also mentioned details regarding the facility. The name of the Opera House's stage electrician, Mr. H. K. Bullock, and a stage carpenter, Mr. Henry Gray, were noted. Also within the same issue a second advertisement was put in by the manager of the Farmville Opera House, J. L. Hart. In his search for bookings Mr. Hart mentioned the seating capacity of 750 seats. This number is unconfirmed, however, because in the same issue a separate listing stated the Opera House had a capacity of 500 seats.[5]

If railroad access was the key to providing entertainment to fill these cultural centers, Farmville was well suited. The Norfolk and Western rail line stopped in Farmville two blocks from the Opera House. This rail line provided direct access to nearby major cities such as Richmond, Charlottesville, Lynchburg, and Roanoke. Advertisements and reviews indicate that the touring companies approached Farmville from every direction and distance in the state. This fact proved valuable in my research because I was able to turn to major newspapers of those cities and sometimes discover more in-depth descriptions of the companies that traveled on to Farmville.

The promotional brochure provided valuable evidence in my attempt to acquire a greater understanding of the Farmville Opera House. Still, visual or textual information of the theatre's interior and stage was lacking. Continued scanning of the issues of the *Farmville Herald* eventually revealed a visual clue, but other investigations into the workings of the theatre and its management led to more frustration and yielded only small discoveries.

I made trips to the town offices of Farmville, hoping that somewhere in their records information on the construction and maintenance during the early years of the building would emerge. My hopes were raised when I was informed that the Farmville Town Council kept meticulous minutes. Since the town built and managed the early years of the Opera House, such minutes could provide clues as to cost and maintenance. The mysterious difficulty in learning about the Opera House continued as I examined the dusty ledgers. The minutes were indeed meticulous, but they began only in 1889, four years after the construction of the Opera House.

Pouring over the handwritten notations did result in some information. Details ranged from the minute notation and ensuing council vote on spending a few dollars for a new lock at the Opera House to the mention in an 1891 meeting of the changeover from gas to electricity in the town buildings. This finding indicates that the Farmville Opera's house and stage lighting was originally from a gas source until 1891.[6]

Physical evidence about the Farmville Opera House proved difficult to find for reasons I have already stated. I tried to find descendants of those connected with the theatre who might be able to provide memorabilia and oral history. I followed leads based on local family names connected with the Opera House, and this led to many telephone conversations with various sons, daughters, grandsons, and granddaughters, ranging from Washington, DC, to Durham, North Carolina. These conversations yielded little new information.

One other frustrating facet of the research was the discovery that the town of Farmville had a local photographer in the early to mid-twentieth century. His photography shop had burned down and with it many of the photos he had taken over the years. It was one more roadblock in the elusive search for tangible evidence regarding this old theatre.

So how to determine what the physical space of the Farmville Opera House was like? What I needed was a general understanding of these small theatres and the types of entertainment that played in them. One of the most popular forms of theatrical entertainment that toured these opera houses in the early twentieth century was the "ten-twenty-thirty" melodramas. Clues to these small theatres and their stages were found in such books as Garrett Leverton's *The Great Diamond Robbery and Other Recent Melodramas.*

Each theater had four or five stock sets of scenery—the cottage interior, the palace set, the prison, the center-door-fancy, and an exterior. Traveling companies fitted their entire repertoire into these stock sets and the theater was packed nightly at admission prices of ten cents for the gallery, twenty cents for the balcony, and thirty cents for seats on the main floor. Actors did vaudeville acts in front of the curtain while between-the-act scene changes were made, and a set of dishes was given away on Saturday night to the lucky number. Throughout the country this theater flourished.[7]

Owing to the relatively inexpensive price of admission, these companies could not afford the exorbitant cost of shipping elaborate physical settings. Theatres such as the Farmville Opera House had to maintain their own stock set of scenery if these popular forms of entertainment were to come. Research revealed that the ten-twenty-thirty melodramas did visit Farmville. The "Old Reliable" Harvey Theater Company spent the week of August 30, 1899, in the town. The company advertised itself as "supporting Willard H. Harvey and Dorothy Lamb in a repertoire of the latest comedy successes. Change of play nightly. Prices—10, 20, 30¢." As an added inducement a special "Bon Bon Matinee" was advertised for Saturday, when each child was presented with a bag of free candy.[8] The Harvey Theater Company was typical of these types of companies, right down to the free bag of candy, similar to the free set of dishes.

Leverton's description, together with the fact that these ten-twenty-thirty melodrama companies toured Farmville, helps to clarify the details seen in the only interior photo of the Farmville Opera House found to date, a 1905 photo that ran in the *Farmville Herald*. The photo was taken from the back of the auditorium looking onto a lighted stage, in front of which stood a young man. On the stage appears to be a setting fitting the description of one of the standard stock set pieces mentioned in the Leverton description of the ten-twenty-thirty theatre companies. The photo shows a rather elaborately painted center door across the back of the stage—a center-door fancy. This flat or drop was most likely a possession the Opera House kept in stock to accommodate the simple needs of touring productions. Closer examination of the photo shows what appears to be a gap, or space, between the two identically painted doors. This would indicate that the set could be pulled apart at the very center. Judging from the space of the stage and its apparent depth, it seems feasible that each half of the scenic unit could easily disappear offstage left or right. Owing to the second-story nature of the Farmville theatre, having the unit rise and disappear above does not seem feasible unless rolled like an Oleo curtain. The exterior line drawing of the building also confirmed that the original theatre had no raised-fly type structure.

The appearance of this stock-type scenic unit does not necessarily confirm that the Opera House, and thus the municipality of Farmville, had its own repertoire of stock scenery. However, if the purpose of having such a facility was to bring culture to the area, then having such scenery in stock would have made it possible to attract the smaller companies, the only ones who could afford to make these small-town stops on their touring circuit. The lack of scenic variety at the Opera House

Interior view of the Farmville Opera House, 1905. Used by permission of the *Farmville Herald*.

can be inferred from the lack of mention of scenic elements in most newspaper reviews and company advertisements printed in the weekly editions of the *Farmville Herald*.

The stage on which the performers entertained looked typical of the time, approximately four to five feet above the floor of the auditorium. This height, and the fact that the Opera House was advertised as a second-floor theatre, suggests the existence of trapdoors. Follow-up examinations of the current building confirmed this. Mathematical scale estimates from the photo indicate that the proscenium opening was approximately twenty-eight feet wide and fourteen feet high. The depth of the stage cannot be accurately determined, but the straight-back chair just right of center stage in the photo provides evidence enough for a reasonably accurate estimation. There is adequate space both above and below this chair.

How to verify guesswork from a less-than-distinct black-and-white photo? Besides researched comparisons with similar theatres and mathematical comparisons based on scale and depth perception, looking at the size of the casts of the shows booked into the Farmville Opera House would give a practical feel for the stage. The largest show discovered was advertised as *The Original Nashville Students Combined with Gideon's Big Minstrel Carnival*. This one-night performance included more than forty-five minstrel stars consisting of twelve comedians, ten solo singers, sixteen dancers, and eight big Oleo acts.[9] Although this gives us no mathematical figures for the size of the stage, it does indicate that the stage, and the theatre itself, was no modest affair. Other booking advertisements confirm an ample staging area.

Determining the types of entertainment that played the stage of the Farmville Opera House proved easy. The local paper covered or advertised troupes that came to Farmville on a weekly basis until it ceased to be a live theatre space around 1910. First there were the "operas" themselves. Operas were confined to two types: (1) presentations of selected songs, or acts, from traditional classic operas or (2) full productions of what were known in the period as comic light operas.

An example of the first type was *Martha*, a production given in the Farmville Opera House on Friday, February 24, 1899. In this engagement Louise Brehany gave "an act of the grand opera." Two advertisements appeared in the *Farmville Herald*. One noted that she "has gained a national reputation through her success with Sousa's Band, the Chicago Marine Band, Edouard Remenyi, [the] Bernard Listemann Company and other great organizations, and this year heads her own company."[10]

Ms. Brehany held some clout. Tickets for her performance were expensive—one dollar for reserved seats and seventy-five cents for general admission. These admission prices were quite high for the time and location. According to advertisements for *Martha*, advance tickets could be purchased at Crute's Drug Store. The significance of this detail is that it indicates that management of the Opera House was most likely limited, without full-time box-office personnel.

An example of the second type of opera, the comic light opera, was *The Mascot*, which played the Farmville Opera House on Tuesday, March 23, 1909, and was performed by the Herald Square Opera Company. This event received an enthusiastic review from the local paper, which called it "an evening of laughter and song." The Herald Square Company was obviously no stranger to Farmville, as this performance was billed as a "Return Engagement." The advertisement alluded to "all the old favorites in the cast and a Chorus Larger Than Ever."[11]

Legitimate stage shows also booked into the Opera House. They ran the gamut, from ten-twenty-thirty melodramas to musical farces and tragedies. In early 1892 *Little Lord Fauntleroy* was presented at the Opera House. This production rode the train into town from its engagement in Richmond two days before. The production was produced by T. Henry French and his New York company. Another example is the melodrama *Tempest and Sunshine*, which was presented by the W. F. Mann Company, with Gertrude Ritchie and Suzanne Ames as the name players. They played the theatre March 29, 1909. This play was a dramatization of a popular novel of the day by Mary J. Holmes.[12]

Not every show that played the Farmville Opera House was song and dance or light entertainment. A temperance drama, William W. Pratt's *Ten Nights in a Bar Room*, was advertised to play the town with the "brilliant little child star" Little Verna Marie.[13] Shakespeare's *Hamlet* played the boards for two nights—November 10 and 11, 1893. This production starred Mr. James Young in the title role. He came to Farmville from an engagement in Charlottesville, Virginia.[14]

A rather well-known actor played the Opera House in April of 1902. Mr. Robert Downing, billed as "America's Tragedian," brought to town his production of Robert Montgomery Bird's *The Gladiator*.[15] This play was the 1831 star vehicle of the famous Edmond Forrest. His portrayal of the play's leading role of Spartacus made *The Gladiator* one of the most popular plays during the middle years of the nineteenth century. Information about Mr. Downing is limited, but his name does appear in many lists of well-known nineteenth-century actors.

Perhaps the most renowned of all nineteenth-century performers came with the presentation of *The Harvest Moon* at the Opera House on February 6, 1892, with its advertised star Fanny Janauschek. Born in Prague, Czechoslovakia, in 1830, she trained at the Prague Conservatory and made quite a name for herself performing the classics in Germany, Austria, and Russia. She came to the United States in 1867 and remained until her death. Fanny Janauschek's greatest American claim was in playing Lady Macbeth with Edmond Booth.[16]

Although small by most standards, the Farmville Opera House in its short existence served its community and its purpose. Leading the way in pubic support for the arts, this small, obscure theatre did what many of its sister opera houses across this country set out to do—bring entertainment to people who might not otherwise have an opportunity to see it. Soon the popularity and inexpensive admission prices of the early movies would supplant live theatre as the entertainment of choice for rural and urban Americans. Theatres such as the venerable Farmville Opera House would be converted to other purposes or demolished. Keeping their memories alive is important to our cultural history. Trying to piece together those that no longer physically exist as theatres, such as the Farmville Opera House, is a worthwhile, but challenging, endeavor.

Notes

1. H. Clarence Bradshaw, *History of Farmville Virginia, 1798–1948* (Farmville, VA: *Farmville Herald*, 1994), 244.

2. H. Clarence Bradshaw, *History of Prince Edward County, Virginia* (Richmond, VA: Dietz Press, 1955), 699.

3. *Brief Historical Review of Prince Edward County* (Prince Edward County, VA: Local publication, 1888), 5.

4. See John W. Frick and Carlton Ward, eds., *Directory of Historic American Theatres* (New York: Greenwood Press, 1987).

5. Julius Cahn, ed., *Julius Cahn's Official Theatrical Guide* (New York: Julius Cahn, 1896), 554.

6. Farmville Council Minutes, 1891, Farmville City Records Town Council Office, Farmville Municipal Building, Farmville, VA.

7. Garrett Leverton, ed., *The Great Diamond Robbery and Other Recent Melodramas* (Bloomington: Indiana University Press, 1963), ix.

8. *Farmville Herald*, Sep. 9, 1899.

9. *Farmville Herald*, Jan. 15, 1899.

10. *Farmville Herald*, Feb. 17, 1899.

11. *Farmville Herald*, March 19, 26, 1909.

12. Bradshaw, *History of Prince Edward County, Virginia*, 164; *Richmond Times-Dispatch*, Jan. 26, 1892; *Farmville Herald*, April 2, 1909.

13. *Farmville Herald*, Feb. 14, 1905.

14. *Farmville Herald*, Nov. 4, 1893.

15. Bradshaw, *History of Farmville*, 164.

16. Ibid.

Contributors

Jane Barnette is an assistant professor in the Department of Theatre and Film at Bowling Green State University, where she teaches theatre history to graduate and undergraduate students. She just finished directing Jean Anouilh's *Antigone* at BGSU, so she feels like she's been walled up in a cave for the last few months. Her essay comes from her current research about the effects of railroads on Chicago-area theatre from 1870 to 1920. When not teaching, serving, or researching, Jane practices yoga and designs (and collects) makeup for stage and screen.

Sarah J. Blackstone is currently dean of Humanities and Fine Arts at California State University, Chico. She has spent her career researching and writing about nineteenth-century American popular entertainment —specifically Buffalo Bill's Wild West. This research has led her to many other areas of study and to wonderful adventures in archives and museums across rural America. Her publications include *The Business of Being Buffalo Bill: Selected Letters of William F. Cody, 1879–1917* and *Buckskins, Bullets, and Business: A History of Buffalo Bill's Wild West.*

J. K. Curry is an associate professor in the Department of Theatre and Dance at Wake Forest University. She is the author of *Nineteenth-Century American Women Theatre Managers* and *John Guare: A Research and Production Sourcebook.*

LaVahn Hoh coauthored, with William J. Rough, *Step Right Up! The Adventure of Circus in America* and produced the video *A Day in the Life of the Clyde Beatty/Cole Brothers Circus.* LaVahn was one of three historians interviewed for the Arts and Entertainment Network documentary, *200 Years of the American Circus* and was also seen on another A&E documentary titled *Daredevils*. He is a professor of drama and associate chair in the Department of Drama at the University of Virginia in Charlottesville. For the past eighteen years, LaVahn has taught the only college accredited course on the American circus, "The History of Circus in America." He has received a grant from the National Endowment for the Arts and a fellowship from the Institute for Advanced Technology in the Humanities at the University of Virginia to create a Web site of the circuses in America from 1793 to the 1940s.

Dawn Larsen grew up in Branson, Missouri. In 1990 she moved to Tennessee to pursue an MA in Communication Arts from Austin Peay State University, where she completed her Toby play and her thesis, "A Continuing History of Toby Shows with an Acknowledgment of the Past and Plans for the Future." This endeavor prompted the informal organization of the Hard Corn Players in 1991. She continued to pursue her love of late-nineteenth-century and early-twentieth-century American folk theatre in her dissertation, "Corn under Canvas: Reconstructing Toby Shows in Tennessee," and received her PhD from Southern Illinois University at Carbondale in 1999. Larsen is currently chair of the Visual and Performing Arts Department and associate professor of theatre and speech at Volunteer State College in Gallatin, Tennessee.

Barbara Lewis, scholar, theatre historian, playwright, and translator, connects her interest in history and her passion for the theatre in her current research, which is focused on lynching and performance. Dr. Lewis, who is director of the William Monroe Trotter Institute for the Study of Black Culture at the University of Massachusetts at Boston, has also published on minstrelsy and African American theatre in the civil rights era. Her writing has appeared in such publications as *The Drama Review*, *Theatre Journal*, *African American Review*, *American Theatre*, and *Callaloo*. Before assuming the directorship of the Trotter Institute, Dr. Lewis was chair of the Department of Theatre at the University of Kentucky.

Elizabeth A. Osborne is a PhD candidate in the Theatre and Performance Studies program at the University of Maryland, College Park. Her areas of interest include early-twentieth-century American theatre, particularly the Federal Theatre Project, arts advocacy, and the reciprocal relationship between theatre and community. In addition to numerous dramaturgical credits, she has written several entries for *The Facts on File Companion to American Drama*, edited by Jackson Bryer and Mary Hartig (New York: Facts on File, 2003); and *The Encyclopedia of African American Literature*, edited by Hans Ostrom and J. David Macey Jr. (New York: Greenwood Press, forthcoming).

kb saine is interim director of theatre at Wesleyan College, where she directs and teaches text analysis, acting, and directing. She earned her MFA in Theatre Pedagogy/Directing from Virginia Commonwealth University. Her research interests include anything that has yet to be documented, especially in areas of racial and gender representation.

Bruce Speas teaches at Longwood University. Former resident director at the Clarence Brown Theatre in Knoxville, Tennessee, he teaches directing, theatre history, and acting. As a playwright his works have been produced on both coasts. His international work includes participation with LaMaMa International in Spoleto and an association with the Ludlow Festival in England.